TALES OF AFGHANISTAN

BY THE SAME AUTHOR

Arabian Fairy Tales
Folk Tales of Central Asia
Tiger of the Frontier
The Tale of the Four Dervishes
The Assemblies of Al-Hariri

TALES OF AFGHANISTAN

by

Amina Shah

THE OCTAGON PRESS
LONDON

Copyright © 1982 by Amina Shah

All rights of reproduction and translation reserved. No part of this publication may be reproduced in any form or by any means, electronic, mechanical or photographic, by recording or any information storage or retrieval system or method now known or to be invented or adapted, without prior permission obtained in writing from The Octagon Press Ltd., 14 Baker Street, London W1M 2HA, England, except by a reviewer to whom a copy has been sent by the publisher for a review written for inclusion in a journal, magazine, newspaper or broadcast.

ISBN: 90086094 4

Photoset, printed and bound in Great Britain by
Redwood Burn Limited
Trowbridge, Wiltshire

CONTENTS

	Page
The Unforgettable Sneeze	7
The Amir who Became a Weaver	10
The Tailor and the Deev	15
Know-All and the Cowardly Thieves	24
The Widow's Son and the Fig-Pecker	30
The Well-Digger and the Deev	42
The King's Favourite and the Beautiful Slave	48
The Princess and the Bulbul	54
The Magic Shawl and the Enchanted Trumpet	60
The Well of Everlasting Life	68
The Ruby Ring	71
The Beggar, the Lion and the Dog	76
The Water-Carrier's Fabulous Sons	83
The Faithful Gazelle	90
The Leopard and the Jinn	96
Prince Mahsud and the King Rat	103
The Amir who was a Beggar	108
The Meatballs' Leader	114

The Unforgettable Sneeze

Once upon a time there lived a man called Akbar who worked as a cook at the Court of the Amir Abdur Rahman.

Now, the Amir was a man of very great generosity, and used to invite many people to eat with him several times a week. Akbar was a good cook, whose speciality was the making of soup. He knew exactly how to make the most delicious concoctions out of the vegetables the Amir loved best. One day, he made a large dish of pea soup, as delicately green as jade, and as sweetly flavoured as the first peas of the season. There were large numbers of guests, all of the highest degree, and servants carried huge platters hither and thither as if their lives depended upon speed, as indeed they did, for once he was seated the Amir Abdur Rahman did not expect to be kept waiting. In came Akbar and placed the huge dish of soup in front of his royal master. The Amir's eyes lit up, his nose caught the delicate scent of the peas, and he smiled. But, a moment later something terrible happened. The cook sneezed into the Amir's soup! With a bellow of rage Abdur Rahman rose up and tipped his dish over onto the spotless white cloth. He pointed at the quivering Akbar and shouted 'Out of this room, out of my kingdom! You are banished from Kabul from this very second!'

All eyes were on the poor cook, who was crawling on all fours out of the dining-hall. All the guests tried to distract the Amir by offering him titbits from other dishes. Out in the kitchen the wretched cook put a few things in a cloth, and ran home. 'Fatima, my dear,' he told his wife. 'I am banished from Kabul for sneezing in the Amir's soup, and I'm lucky to escape with my life. I will go to my uncle in Pul'i'Kumri until this has all blown over.'

'But ... but,' wept Fatima, 'How long will that be, do you think? You know what a terrible temper the Amir has, he might have you flogged when you return!'

'Well, I must just stay away until the scandal has died down,' said Akbar. 'Take the money I have buried under the floor to live on whilst I am away. I'll send you more when I can get a job somewhere else.' So they said goodbye and he ran off as fast as his legs would carry him.

Soon the tale of how Akbar had sneezed right into the Amir's soup was doing the round of the bazaars, and people laughed behind their hands to think of such a thing happening right at the Amir's table. Fatima managed to do some embroidery for a rich woman's family, and so, taking a little now and again from the store of money under the floor, she did not suffer much hardship. But of course she missed Akbar, and longed for his return. The months went by and she at last heard from him, and a year passed, then two. When the third year since Akbar had fled to his uncle's house was just beginning, Fatima, always hopeful, sent Akbar a letter by a traveller, begging him to return. She said she was sure that the Amir had forgotten about the sneeze, and that he really should try and return home to Kabul. People seemed to have forgotten to gossip about Akbar and the pea soup, and she added that she, too, would like him to return so that their son, born after his father's disappearance, might at least know that he had a father.

As soon as Akbar got this letter, he realized that he was being cowardly to remain out of sight so long.

He would go back to Kabul, take up his old friends again, and enjoy home life once more. Poor Fatima, he thought, she should not be left to bring up the child by herself, it was not right. 'Uncle,' said he, 'I am going back to Kabul; there is not likely to be any more gossip about me there after these three years. I have the boy to think about, after all. So, thank you for letting me stay all this time, but I must leave tomorrow at dawn.'

His uncle bade him farewell, with many blessings, and they went to bed. Next day, as soon as the sun rose, Akbar took his few belongings in a small pack, and set off for Kabul. He was lucky enough to fall in with some Nomads who let him ride on a camel part of the way. After that he walked for a day or two, then met up with an old man driving some donkeys. 'Father,' said he, 'Let me help you with these animals, in exchange for a ride now and again.' The old man agreed, and at long last, Akbar arrived in Kabul. Saying goodbye to the donkey drover, Akbar went to get a drink of water from a well not far from his home. He took a deep drink, and washed his hands and face. Then, he heard two women talking, as they filled their water jars. 'Let me see, now, how old is little Nadir?' asked one, putting down her jar. 'Oh, two and a half years old, maybe three,' the other replied. 'He was born about the time that Akbar the Cook sneezed in the Amir's pea soup!'

The Amir who Became a Weaver

Once upon a time there was an Amir who used to go through the streets of his capital city disguised as a traveller, listening to what his people thought, in order to help them. If he found there was great suffering in any family he would leave some money at their door, and do good by stealth in every way he could.

One evening, with his faithful Vizir beside him, he was sitting in a café drinking tea with some merchants, when one said:

'May Allah give everlasting life to our noble Amir, but his existence must indeed be devoid of any interest, when he has no trade but that of being an Amir.'

'Why do you think that?' the disguised monarch wanted to know, with a glance at his Vizir.

'Just think of it, nothing but meetings of the Council, affairs of State, great feasts and visits from foreigners who want something; His Majesty's life must be sometimes quite boring,' continued the merchant, and the others in the room agreed.

'What do you think the Amir should do about it?' asked the Vizir, trying to control his temper.

'Why, learn a trade, of course!' said the merchant, and the others all laughed. 'But seriously, if he could become interested in something which he could do with his hands, his life would be much more interesting, I assure you.'

'You are right,' said the Amir, 'a man should have a trade at his finger-tips, in case he might be in need of it one day, even if he be of royal blood.' And he smiled as he sipped his green tea, for a thought was forming in his mind.

When they returned to the Palace that night the Vizir said:

'O, Fountain of Knowledge and Well of Wisdom, if you wish me to take action against that man and his companions who spoke so carelessly of their ruler, let me go now, and I shall have them in prison before day-break.' His eyes were bright with anger, and his beard wagged like a goat's as he spoke.

But the Amir raised his hand in admonition.

'No, my dear Vizir, stay your wrath, for my outspoken subjects have indeed given me something to think about. Tomorrow summon to the Court all the coppersmiths, carpet-makers, potters, dyers and other tradesmen, so that I may choose one of their crafts and learn it. The merchant was right, I need to do something with my hands.'

Next day all the craftsmen were assembled, and the Amir watched each one at his own specific trade, until he saw the beautiful workmanship for which the city was famous in those days. After looking at everything very carefully, the Amir decided to become proficient in the art of the weaver. So the finest weaver in all the land was sent to the Palace each day to teach the Amir, until he had completely mastered the art.

Whenever he needed to have a fresh outlook on a problem, or relax completely after arguments with his ministers, the Amir would work at his loom until he had forgotten all the cares of the day.

He had one especial design of which he was very fond, a colourful flower border which he wove to perfection, and he made several small silk squares of this motif which he presented to the Queen and her ladies as a mark of favour.

One day, when the Amir and the Vizir were wandering (disguised as merchants) down a particularly dark street, two men who had been following them suddenly pounced, and brought both the Amir and his minister to the ground. They dragged them into a sinister-looking house nearby, with darkened shutters, and tied them up inside one of the rooms.

'What a lucky chance' said one evil robber to the other, as they examined the gold in the two purses stolen from their prisoners. 'We can buy ourselves some new clothes with this and be taken for gentlemen. But what shall we do with these men?'

'Let us alone', said the Vizir, thinking quickly. 'We have done you no harm. We are weavers, coming from Samarkand to weave tapestries at the Court of the Amir. If you kill us, you will lose a lot of money. You wouldn't like to do that, would you?'

'How is that?' asked the first robber, greedy for more gold. 'Explain at once, or you will feel my dagger!'

'My companion here', continued the Vizir calmly, 'is so skilled in weaving that he can command a thousand gold pieces for a handkerchief.'

'What!' cried the second robber, 'Then weave one, and we shall take it and sell it in the city.' And they untied the Amir, giving him back his small hand loom which he had been carrying with him.

The handkerchief which the Amir now proceeded to make took three days. When it was finished, it was the most beautiful piece of work that the Amir had ever done, and he gave it to the robbers with these words:

'This is worthy of the Queen herself—take it to the Palace and offer it to one of the ladies of the Court for Her Majesty, and you can command a thousand gold pieces for it ... I swear upon my life!'

While one robber went off to sell the handkerchief, the other watched that the two prisoners did not escape. Wearing new clothes, and posing as a foreign merchant with silk goods of inestimable value, the first robber gained access to the outer door of the Harem, and sent in the handkerchief to be shown to the Queen.

No sooner had Her Majesty set eyes on the design which had been created by the Amir himself, and examined the craftsmanship, than she knew it was the work of her husband. She, and she alone, knew that the Amir was missing, for in case the country should be taken over by enemies, the news of the ruler's disappearance was known by none other.

'Who brings this handkerchief?' she asked her lady-in-waiting.

'Your Majesty, it is a foreign merchant who is asking a thousand pieces of gold for it. He says he has brought it from a far country.'

'Buy it, give him what he asks, but have him secretly followed,' ordered the Queen, 'and bring me back complete directions of the place at which he is staying. Also, ask him if he can bring any more like this.'

The go-between did as she was told. When the robber received the gold pieces without any haggling on the part of the Harem woman, he went back to his associate as fast as his legs would carry him.

'Brother, we are in luck,' said he, 'for they gave me the money right away, and asked if we had any more like it, so we can get this fellow to weave more.'

'Excellent,' said the other rogue, 'We will get him to make another ten of these, and then we can kill him.'

As soon as the Queen received the information from the Chief Spy regarding the whereabouts of the robbers' house, she sent for the Captain of the Guard, and told him all she knew.

'Thus,' she finished, 'it is obvious your soldiers must storm that house, for no doubt the Amir is held prisoner there. Pray Allah you will find him in good health!'

'To hear is to obey, your Majesty,' barked the Captain of the Guard, and gathering his troops, set out for the place at once.

While the Amir was beginning to weave the second handkerchief, the two robbers were counting their gold, and so it was a complete surprise to them when the soldiers burst into the house half an hour later. The Amir was never more pleased to see his soldiers in all his life, and led the way back to the Palace with a joyful tread.

Alas, the two robbers, for all their fine clothes, had their heads struck from their shoulders, and their store of gold was distributed among the poor.

Happily reunited with his Queen, and praising her for her cleverness in understanding the meaning of the cryptic message he had woven into the handkerchief, the Amir ruminated:

'Yes, indeed, it is perfectly true that everyone should learn a trade, for little does he know when he might have need of it, even if he be an Amir!'

The Tailor and the Deev

Once upon a time there was a handsome young tailor, who came from Kandahar, and who wanted to go to sea, as he had spent nearly all his life at home. At the time of which I speak, he took passage in a fine ship, which was taking fine carpets to India, when a great storm sprang up and the ship was wrecked. When the tailor, whose name was Hamid, opened his eyes in the morning after the storm, he found himself cast up on a small island which appeared to be uninhabited by humans, although there were hundreds of sea-birds nesting on the rocks. Being very hungry, Hamid ate several of the eggs and then set off on a tour of the island. As far as he could see, there was nothing but a bare rock-strewn landscape, and after cutting his feet, he decided to give up the search. In a rocky pool beside him, he started to dig with his fingers, as he thought he saw something glittering, and took out what appeared to be a large shell. With his scissors, which had been saved because they were hanging on a leather thong at his waist, he levered the shell open, and to his surprise he saw inside a very small creature the size of his thumb and growing bigger every moment. The shell dropped from his fingers, there was a roaring noise in his ears, and a huge Deev stood before him. It looked like a skeleton, dressed in some sort of white transparent material.

'How dare you rouse me from my age-long rest? In that shell I have slept for a thousand years!' howled the Deev, in a voice like a dozen fiends wailing together. 'Come, and I will crush you like a flea, you wretched human.'

'No! No! Do not do that!' shouted Hamid as loud as he could, 'And I will give you anything you ask.'

'And what are *you* likely to be able to give, may I ask?' shrieked the Deev.

'Well, if I am rescued I will give you one whole gold coin,' said Hamid, for this to him seemed a great fortune.

'That is nothing to me', growled the Deev. 'I need nothing that money can buy.'

'Well, what do you suggest?' asked Hamid.

'I want your soul', the Deev responded, 'for I have lost mine long, long ago, and if you give me yours, then you can go free.'

'I will give it to you as soon as I am rescued', said Hamid, for he knew that the Deev could not take his soul from him by force, it must be given willingly by his own consent.

'All right then,' said the Deev sulkily, 'Here is a ship coming, get on board, and let us have an end of this argument.'

Hamid was so excited that he stood and waved his arms, jumping up and down on the rocks. He completely forgot about the Deev, which had made itself invisible when the sailors from the ship brought a boat to the island in response to Hamid's signals of distress. All the crew crowded round Hamid, asking him about his story, which they thought a great adventure. But Hamid did not mention the Deev, for he was afraid of being laughed at. The Deev had made itself invisible in order to follow Hamid wherever he went, for it was determined to be possessed of Hamid's soul.

The ship which had rescued him put Hamid off at the nearest port. He wanted to get a job as soon as he could, because he had nothing in the world, and tailoring was the only trade he knew. He wandered about the seaport town, with a few coins that the crew of the ship had collected amongst themselves for him, looking for a chance to get back to sea.

Now, it chanced that the King's daughter was coming back from a journey to India, to visit her sister who had married a nobleman at the Court of the Grand Moghal, and she dropped her golden purse as she stepped into the curtained palanquin which was to convey her. As the black slaves moved off with the poles of their young mistress's litter on their stout shoulders, they kicked up the dust, and the purse was covered. Thus it was that Hamid, stubbing his toe, looked down and seeing something glitter picked up the beautiful golden purse. He was turning it over in his hands when one of the Princess's servants came back to look for it.

She cried out as she saw it in Hamid's hands:

'Thief! Thief! How dare you steal a purse belonging to the daughter of the King! Give it back at once, the guards will take you to prison for this!', and as the guards came running, she pointed out Hamid as the thief who had stolen her mistress's golden purse. It was useless for the poor tailor to protest his innocence. He was overpowered and taken to prison, where he was thrown into a narrow cell with one small window. Days passed, and he was only given bread and water to eat, so soon he was very thin and pale.

One night when he could not sleep, and was sitting on the floor of his cell, wondering whatever was to become of him the Deev appeared in front of him.

'You tricked me!' shouted the Deev, 'You said you would give me your soul when you were rescued, but you forgot all about it, didn't you? Now look at the state you are in. You might as well give me your soul while you can, for soon you will be starved to death, and what good will your soul be to you then?'

Hamid thought very hard. He did not want to give

up his soul yet awhile, for he hoped that there might be some chance for him to prove his innocence when he came before the Kadi's court.

'I will give you my soul the day I marry the King's daughter,' he said, to try and get rid of the Deev for at least some time. Marrying the daughter of the King was the very last thing in the world that he thought possible, for was he not in prison, accused of stealing from Her Royal Highness?

'All right then,' said the Deev eagerly, for it did have some magic powers, 'I will help you, and I expect you to give me your soul for all the trouble you have brought me in rousing me from my long, long sleep.'

The jailer with clinking keys was unlocking the door of Hamid's stuffy little cell. The Deev made itself invisible.

'Unhappy tailor!' cried the jailer, 'Now is your time, for you are to be brought before the Kadi to answer for your disgraceful crime of stealing from our beloved King's favourite daughter. And he gave the poor young man a shove and led him out into the daylight.

Now, an honest woman had seen the purse drop from the Princess's palanquin, and having heard that a foreign tailor was held in prison accused of stealing it, she went to the house of the Kadi, and, pulling at his cloak, said:

'The young tailor accused of stealing the purse belonging to our beloved King's daughter is innocent, for I saw with my own eyes the Princess drop it, and no sooner had this unfortunate young man picked it up than the guards seized him, as the Princess's servant was shrieking "Thief! Thief!"'

'Good woman,' responded the Kadi, 'rest assured that I will release the young man. Blessings upon you for your testimony.' And he set off for the court.

Hamid's heart fell when he was led before the

Kadi, who asked him to tell his story of what had happened.

'I stubbed my foot on the purse, hidden as it was in the dust, your Honour,' said Hamid, 'and picked it up. I did not steal it, as Allah is my witness.'

The Kadi smiled, and inclined his head.

'Owing to the testimony of a poor and honest woman who has just spoken to me in your defence,' said he kindly, 'you are released, and I am satisfied that you are innocent. Go in peace. You are to be given some money to help you on your way.'

Then Hamid was happy once more, and went to find a tea-house where he could have a cup of tea to celebrate the return of his liberty.

No sooner was he out of the Court, than the voice of the Deev said in his ear:

'Now that I have arranged your release, start getting a job at the Court of the King, for you remember that you promised me your soul when you married the King's daughter, and I cannot wait for ever!'

Hamid agreed, and knowing that he could not work at tailoring at the Palace, he went to the royal kitchens and got a job as a scullion. After a while, as he had worked so well, he was promoted to the position of junior cook, and soon became a waiter at the royal feasts. Little by little he was climbing the ladder of success, until he was Sherbet-Carrier to the King himself. Much of this promotion was, of course, due to the magical influence of the Deev who appeared from time to time as Hamid's career progressed.

'Not long now before the Princess sees you,' said the Deev one night, with a harsh, mirthless laugh, appearing beside Hamid's bed when he was just going to sleep. After it had disappeared, Hamid was unable to close his eyes. His long-haired Angora cat lay on a cushion and watched her master with her beautiful amber eyes. To Hamid's surprise, the cat spoke.

'Master, master,' said she in the human tongue, 'Have no fear about the Deev, for when the time comes for it to demand your soul, I shall deal with it for you.' And she licked her long fluffy grey fur delicately.

'Why, what is the plan?' asked Hamid eagerly, 'Tell me all you have in mind, omitting nothing.'

'Not yet,' said the cat. 'When the time comes I will tell you.'

So Hamid had to be satisfied with that. He fell asleep soon afterwards, and when he woke next day he wondered if indeed he had dreamed the whole thing, for the Angora cat showed no inclination to speak to him again. When he stroked her fur and spoke to her, she merely stalked away with fluffy tail held high.

Next day, there was a wonderful State Banquet, and Hamid, in his velvet tunic and silken trousers, which he had made for himself as soon as he could get the material, waited upon his royal master and the foreign guests so well that the Princess, who was watching the proceedings with the ladies of the harem from behind a lattice screen, fell head over heels in love with him. She sent her old nurse to the King next day to tell her father that she would marry the young Sherbet-Carrier or nobody else in the whole world. The King was very annoyed, and bade his Grand Vizir reason with the Princess and tell her that a Princess of royal blood could never marry a humble Sherbet-Carrier at her father's Court, however handsome he might be. No sooner had the Grand Vizir told the Princess this, than she fell at his feet in a faint, and all the Royal Doctors could not bring her to her senses, though they tried every remedy under the sun. Her case appeared to be hopeless and incurable.

Hamid, unaware of all this, was sitting in his apartment, stroking the fur of his amber-eyed Angora cat, when the Deev appeared before him and said:

'Hamid, your time is nearly come, and soon you shall be the son-in-law of the King. Remember your promise'. Then the Deev gave a harsh triumphant cry and vanished.

'Now is the time for me to speak again, dear Master,' said the cat in the human tongue. 'When you are married to the Princess, as indeed you soon shall be, owing to the Deev's magical powers in this direction—which it has used for its own ends, of course—ask the Deev to prove its prowess in magic by turning into a mouse, and leave the rest to me.' So saying, she closed her golden eyes and fell fast asleep.

At that moment the Grand Vizir came to Hamid's apartment and brought him a command from the King himself to appear at once in Court. In great amazement, Hamid followed the Grand Vizir to the throne-room, where the ruler sat in state on an alabaster throne. On a silken divan placed in the middle of the throne-room lay the Princess, the King's favourite daughter, deep in a death-like trance. The courtiers stood in a wide circle round the divan, sorrow written on every face.

'All the most learned doctors at the Court have been unable to wake my daughter,' said the King, as Hamid came in and bowed before the throne. 'If you can rouse her from this strange sleep, you shall have her hand and half my kingdom, or be put to death in a very painful manner, for I have learned that you are the cause of her fainting in the first place.'

'Your Imperial Majesty!' cried Hamid in horror, throwing himself at the King's feet, 'I swear that I have not seen the Princess except the day that she dropped her golden purse on the quayside. How then could I be the cause of her trance-like state?'

'Do not dare to argue with your King', shouted the ancient grey-bearded Grand Vizir, giving Hamid a blow with his gem-studded stick, 'for the Princess herself has told us that if she did not marry you, she would not allow herself to be given to anyone else in the world!'

Hamid got to his feet and approached the beautiful, pale Princess as she lay on the divan, with everyone in the throne-room watching him like hawks. He looked upon the sleeping face of the Princess and touched her brow with his finger-tips. At that moment the Princess opened her almond eyes and sat up. Then, seeing that she was being observed by Hamid and then the whole Court, veiled herself instantly and rising from the divan, stood in front of her royal father, who was overcome with joy. 'Take my daughter, you have won her', said the King.

So Hamid and the Princess were joined in marriage and there was much rejoicing in the land.

Suddenly there was a roaring in Hamid's ears and the voice of the Deev came loud and clear:

'I claim your soul, for you are now married to the King's daughter.'

Remembering the Angora cat's words, Hamid said:

'Come into the private apartment and I will talk to you', and he felt the Deev pushing past him into the splendidly furnished room where everything was prepared for the young couple. Then Hamid said to his bride:

'Wait for me in the throne-room; I have something to attend to before I can enjoy the celebrations.'

'Give me your soul, for I cannot wait a moment longer!' cried the Deev, hovering in the air and peering at Hamid with his red-rimmed eyes, 'for I have arranged all this by my powers of magic, in order that you should hand over your soul to me today.'

'Powers of magic?' laughed Hamid, for the Angora cat had told him what to say. 'What powers of magic? All that has happened to me is my own Kismet. How can you prove that you are possessed of magical powers?'

'Of course I can!' roared the Deev, 'I can turn myself into anything under the sun, anything, I say! Just ask me and I will do it.'

'Could you turn yourself into a mouse? No, I'm sure you could not!' said Hamid.

'A mouse? A mouse? Why, that is nothing, I will do that before you could count one,' and, suiting action to word, the Deev disappeared, and there was a small mouse running round in circles on the floor.

At that moment the grey cat, which had been hiding behind a curtain, sprang out and swallowed the mouse. Hamid gave a shout of laughter, knowing he was free at last.

'That is the end of the Deev, Master,' said the cat in the human tongue, and slowly closed her amber eyes.

'Oh, my beautiful Angora cat, you shall feed from a golden dish for the rest of your days, and lie always upon none but silken cushions!' promised Hamid with joy, and he was as good as his word.

The dreadful Deev was never seen again, and Hamid and the Princess lived happily ever afterwards.

When the King died, leaving no son, Hamid became the king after him, and under his wise rule all parts of the kingdom were united in peace and prosperity. And all this happened in the days when talking cats came from Angora, and tailors could become kings.

Know-All and the Cowardly Thieves

Once upon a time there lived a man called Fakhri who was always saying that he knew everything. This was a great joke in the whole town, and people used to call after him in the street:

'O, Know-All, how wonderful it must be to know everything!'

Fakhri was so vain he really believed that they admired him, and he preened himself when he heard these words.

One night twenty thieves dressed themselves in red silk trousers, green shirts and golden waistcoats embroidered with silver, as worn by the servants of the Amir. Then they went to the Palace and stole a lot of treasure, jewelled cups and valuable vases, pretending that they were taking them to be cleaned. When the robbery was discovered, the Amir was furious, and caused all his servants to be beaten on the soles of the feet for permitting the theft.

'Find the thieves!' shouted the Amir. 'Bring them to justice, and restore my valuables, or heads will roll!'

'Oh, Protector of the Faithful!' said the Captain of the Guard, 'We have searched high and low for the rogues, but to no avail. Give us one month, your Majestic Presence, and my soldiers and I will run the thieves to ground.'

'So be it', said the Amir, and the Captain of the Guard hastened from the Palace.

Now, he had heard of Fakhri the Know-All, and he knocked on the door of his house. The servant, with much bowing and deep obeisance, admitted the splendid Captain to his master's study, where Fakhri was reading an ancient manuscript.

'O Know-All!' said the Captain of the Guard, 'I have heard of your fame, and have come to consult you.'

'Why, Excellence,' cried Fakhri, 'Consult me upon what subject?'

'There is a band of twenty robbers,' continued the Captain, 'and, dressed as members of his Majesty's household staff, they have had the insolence to steal some valuables of our royal master. Now, you, who know everything, will you tell me who these rogues are?'

'Yes, yes, that I know,' said Fakhri, for he had heard gossip in the bazaar, 'but it is going to be very difficult to find them, for they are extremely dangerous rascals, and known only as the Twenty Thieves.'

'Then you must find where they live, and lead me to them, so that I may recover the Amir's jewelled cups and vases. Otherwise, if you do not do so, your life will be forfeit,' the Captain barked in a very military manner.

'My ... my life?' said poor Fakhri, 'Well, in that case I suppose I must. But how long may I have to find them?'

'You have but twenty days,' said the Captain. 'If, by the end of that time you do not bring the information to me, your head will be struck from your shoulders.'

'I hear, and shall most certainly bring the information you require, O Most Excellent Captain,' replied Fakhri, with an assurance which he did not feel. 'In twenty days, then, you shall see me at the Palace.'

When the Captain had gone Fakhri called his wife and said:

'My dear, something terrible has happened. Because I always know everything, the Captain of the Guard wants me to find out where the Twenty Thieves live, and where they have hidden the Amir's valuables which they stole.'

'And do you know this?' she asked.

'No, I do not, and as he has given me twenty days in which to find them (before my head is struck from my shoulders), I have only twenty days of life left.'

'What shall we do?' she wept, seeing that he was in earnest.

'Get a basket, put into it twenty stones, and each night throw one out of the window, so that I may keep a tally of the time remaining to me. When the twentieth stone is left in the basket, that will be my last day, and I shall put all my affairs in order to await the arrival of the Amir's soldiers.'

His wife cried bitterly, and advised him to flee, but Fakhri knew he could never escape the vengeance of the Amir.

'Just do as I say, Wife,' said he, and continued reading his manuscript.

So, having found twenty pebbles of about the same shape and size, the unhappy woman threw the first from the window that night, saying as it fell:

'That is the first of the twenty.'

Now, as chance would have it, outside the window stood one of the band of Twenty Thieves, listening to hear if the people in the house were at home, for he was thinking of robbing it. The pebble hit him in the eye, and he heard the woman say:

'That is the first of the twenty!'

The thief fled, and went down to the cellar where the rogues held their secret meetings. He said to the chief of the band:

'As I was standing outside the window of the house of Fakhri the Know-All, his wife threw a stone at me from the window, saying:

'"There is the first of the twenty!" I tell you, we must escape from the town, for they will be coming to get us.'

'Nonsense, idiot!' shouted the leader of the robbers, 'You have imagined the whole business.'

'I have not, by the Beard of the Prophet,' swore the thief, 'I heard her say it, and she hit me in the eye with a small stone.'

'Abdul,' said the chief of the robbers to another of the rogues, 'You go outside the house tomorrow night and listen and see if you can hear anything.'

Next night the second thief went outside the house of Fakhri the Know-All and listened. Sure enough, the woman came to the window, opened the shutter and threw out a stone, saying as she did so:

'That is the second of the twenty!'

In fright, the thief ran back to the cellar and told the chief of the band:

'By my Faith, it is indeed true, the wife of Fakhri the Know-All threw a pebble at me and said:

'"That is the second of the twenty!" Valiant Leader, I say we should flee, for if he and his household know about us, we are all dead men.'

'No, do not be foolish!' cried the thief. 'Tomorrow night Amin shall go, for he has the sharpest ears of you all, and I will settle this matter when he brings his report.

But sure enough, when Amin the Thief listened at the shutter, he also was hit on the head by a stone and heard the woman saying:

'This is the third of the twenty!' He, too, returned to the chief with a frightened face.

'Master,' said he, 'We must fly for our lives, for as both Abdul and Hamid have related, the matter of our robbery is known to Fakhri and his wife, and they know the minute we appear, even in the dark!'

'Enough!' roared the chief of the robbers, 'I will go to the great Know-All myself, and make a bargain with him.' So he cloaked himself to the eyes, attended by several of his men, and arrived at Fakhri's door.

Inside, all was quiet, for Fakhri and his wife had gone to bed, and when the chief of the robbers knocked it was some time before the door was opened.

'I expect you know me, my friend,' said the chief, 'Please let me come in, for I have a proposition to make.'

'Certainly, enter,' said Fakhri, not understanding who his visitor might be, but behaving as if he knew all about it.

'Now, let me come straight to the point,' said the chief, 'We are the band of Twenty Thieves, and of course, as you know, we have the Amir's valuables in our cellar. If we give you the things back, will you let us go to another town, and so save our lives? For this kindness we will give you this purse of gold,' and he pressed into Fakhri's hand a heavy leather bag.

'Certainly, certainly,' said Fakhri quickly, and he was much relieved, for he had at first feared the thieves were going to rob his house of his few possessions. 'If you give me the Amir's treasures I shall see that they are returned to the Palace, and I swear nobody will know anything about you.'

'Excellent,' said the chief, 'Tomorrow, then, my men shall leave the sacks containing the treasure outside your house here, on our way to another town.'

They shook hands upon this agreement, and the robber chief went away with his rogues.

Next day, at dawn, there were three heavy sacks outside the house. When Fakhri and his wife opened them, the Amir's jewelled cups and golden vases were within.

'Praises be to Allah!' cried Know-All. 'Come, wife, load these sacks on to the donkey, we are off to the Palace.'

When Fakhri and his loaded donkey arrived at the Palace and asked for the Captain of the Guard, the servants laughed at him and tried to send him away again.

'We cannot ask the Captain of the Guard to see you!' they laughed, 'You are Fakhri the Know-All, trying to play some trick upon his Excellency.'

'No, no, let me speak to him, for I have here all the treasure of the Amir which was stolen by the Twenty Thieves,' said Fakhri. The servants laughed even more loudly.

Now the Grand Vizir was entering the Palace at that moment, and heard the clamour. Then, when he saw that the stolen valuables were indeed in the sacks, he caused Fakhri to be admitted to the presence of the Amir himself, to be thanked by the sovereign in a most fitting manner.

Fakhri found himself the proud possessor of a robe of honour, six black slaves and six white slaves, and had his mouth filled with gold by the Royal Treasurer.

And that is the end of the tale of Know-All and the Twenty Thieves, which just goes to show that it is not really necessary to know everything in order to succeed in life.

The Widow's Son and the Fig-Pecker

Once upon a time there lived a poor village woman, a widow, who had so many children that she could not feed them properly, and as each boy grew big enough, she sent him into the city of Kabul to earn his living. When the time came for her seventh son, Abdulla, to do so, she wept more than usual, for he was her heart's favourite, the light of her eyes.

'My son,' said she, amid her tears, 'Look after yourself, and take care of this magic talisman which I will put round your neck. It will save you from Afrits and Deevs and may Allah have you in His safe keeping!' So saying, she tied a small leather bag round his neck, and watched him out of sight.

When Abdulla got to Kabul he was overawed by the crowds of people, the camels with jingling bells on their necks, and donkeys with necklaces of blue beads. He had brought a piece of rope with him from his village, in order to hire himself out as a porter, as his brothers had done. He was waiting in the market place, where all those who wished to be hired were standing about, when an old woman dressed in black, and heavily veiled but with one eye showing, came up to him.

'Are you hiring yourself as a porter?' she asked, looking at his broad shoulders and strong legs.

'Yes, mistress,' said he, 'I will be happy to serve you. What would you like me to carry?'

'Hush, that I cannot tell you in public. Follow me, and I will take you where we may talk privately.' So saying, she veiled herself completely and Abdulla took up his piece of rope and followed her through the crowded bazaar at a respectful distance.

They went a little way, the woman stopped and looked behind her, then, when she was sure that Abdulla was still in sight, she continued. Taking narrow alleys left and right, they at last emerged on to a broad highway, where a huge walled house was to be seen. In the wall there was a door, with a heavy knocker on it, shaped like an eagle made of brass. The woman stopped, and knocked three times upon the door. Instantly they were admitted by a servant, and Abdulla looked about him with great interest. They were standing in a square blue-tiled courtyard, where fountains played and white doves fluttered from the windows of a turquoise-studded dovecot. The house was evidently that of a rich and noble family and Abdulla was pleased. He thought his first job was going to be very well paid. The old woman led him up a staircase to another door, which she opened with a large key. The room which they then entered was hung with silken curtains of great price. Wooden chests inset with silver and brass stood here and there, and there was a most valuable carpet on the floor. On a silver perch in the window there was a small bird, with drab brown feathers and lack-lustre eyes.

'Know, young man,' began the old woman, 'that this is the house of a rich and beautiful lady, who refused to marry a wicked Magician of evil aspect who saw her one day when she was shopping at the silversmith's bazaar. He was so angered when this lady, my poor mistress, laughed at him, that he turned her into a Fig-Pecker, and there you can see she remains to this day in the guise of a brown bird.' Abdulla looked at the Fig-Pecker with sympathy, and wondered why he should have been brought in to be told about it. The old woman was speaking again:

'After five years of unhappiness, my mistress has

heard that there is a way to cause the spell to be lifted from her, so she sent me to the market today to find someone suitable to help.'

'And am I that person?' asked Abdulla, as the old woman paused in her narrative.

'Yes,' said she, 'and if you will bear with me a bit longer I will tell you all about it.'

'No, Ayesha,' said the bird on the perch, speaking in the language of humans, 'Let me tell the young man myself, for I can see that he is of a sympathetic nature. Go and get him some sweet sherbet to drink, and bring me a fig, for I think I have a little appetite now.'

Abdulla was amazed to hear the Fig-Pecker speak, but he composed himself and sat down upon a cushion which the old woman indicated before she left the room.

The bird, still sitting upon the perch in the window, addressed him.

'Know, young man,' said she in a soft musical voice, 'that the plan I am about to put before you is the only way in which I may be returned to human form, and if you can help me I shall certainly pay you any sum you ask, for I can no longer bear to be confined in the body of a feathered Fig-Pecker!'

Abdulla was just about to laugh, as it seemed to him a very amusing matter, but he managed to restrain his mirth, for the bird was continuing.

'There is, in a certain part of the Blue Water of Bundi-Amir, a deep cavern, and if someone could swim under the water and reach it, the jar containing the Perfume of Enchantment, which is decorated with two miniature horse's heads, is there for the taking. This perfume will restore me to my own shape.'

'The Perfume of Enchantment? How shall I get it for you? I do not know where to go.' said Abdulla.

'You will be told where to go. First you leave here

by the Western Gate at daybreak, then you speak to an old man just outside the gate, who will give you a donkey. By midday you will reach a small caravanserai. There you must seek out the Green-turbanned Doctor, who will give you an enchanted tunic which will save you from being drowned in the deep waters of that certain part of Lake Bundi-Amir to which you should go.'

'B ... but how can I remember all these directions?' stammered Abdulla. 'Suppose I forget something on the way and get lost completely?'

'There is no fear of that,' said the bird, 'for I will have my servant put a magic potion in your drink of sherbet so that all that you have been told here will be fixed indelibly in your mind, and will come to you just when you need it.'

'Say on, Lady,' said Abdulla, 'how am I to find the jar once I get into the underwater cavern?'

'Patience, young man,' said the old woman softly, returning with a glass of sherbet, which she placed before him. 'Everything will be explained to you by a Good Peri, a fairy, who shall speak into your ear each time you have to do anything.'

'Shall I be able to see this Peri?' cried Abdulla.

'No, no,' said the bird, 'you will not be able to see her, for she is made of air, and has no form which can be recognized by man, but the voice will be audible to you and you only. Therefore, heed the voice, and do exactly as it tells you.' Abdulla raised the sweet ice-cold sherbet drink to his lips and drained the glass. After a few moments he felt a peculiar sensation, and heard the bird saying to him as from a great distance:

'Go in peace, young man, and a thousand blessings upon you. When you return with the magic perfume, you shall have as much gold as you wish.'

'Thank you, Lady,' Abdulla found himself replying, as the room began to get more and more hazy to his eyes. The old woman helped him from the room, and then he knew no more.

When he got his senses back, he was lying on the ground outside the wall of the house where he had seen the enchanted Fig-Pecker, and as he was wondering what to do next, a voice said in his ear in the sweetest of tones, 'Abdulla, Abdulla, take your piece of rope and go to the Western Gate, for it is nearly daybreak.'

It was the voice of the Good Peri and Abdulla got to his feet and made his way to the Western Gate by asking an old man, who was going that way, if he could accompany him. Abdulla heard a clicking noise as he was walking along, and putting his hand in his pocket he realized that the old woman must have put some silver coins there. He thanked the man who had told him the way, and walked right out of the Western Gate. Sure enough, as the bird had said, there was a donkey waiting there. An ancient Dervish in a patched cloak was sitting beside the donkey. As soon as he saw the young man he called out:

'Here is the donkey you have to take. Put your piece of rope round its neck as a halter and ride it away.' Abdulla tried to thank the Dervish, but when he looked at him he saw that the old man had closed his eyes in sleep.

'What am I to do now?' said Abdulla to himself, drumming his heels against the donkey's sides as it took him along the dusty road. At that moment the voice of the Good Peri said in his ear:

'Keep to this road until you get to a caravanserai. Then we will meet the Green-turbanned Doctor.'

'Ah, yes,' said Abdulla, and he remembered what the Fig-Pecker had told him. It was a beautiful morning, with the rosy streaks of dawn in the sky, and he began to feel that life was going to be one long adventure. With the money that he would get for finding the precious jar for the enchanted bird he would go home and build a fine house for his mother. Then he would buy new clothes, get himself a pair of leather boots... He stopped dreaming, for the voice of the Good Peri was once more breaking into his thoughts.

'Here is a part of the road where a Demon, a Deev, of most terrible aspect lives in a well,' said the voice in his ear. 'Hold tight on to the talisman which your mother gave you, for it is just going to look out of the well and may frighten the donkey into running away.'

Just as the voice finished speaking, a huge head was thrust up out of the well beside the road, and Abdulla held on to his talisman with one hand. The Demon began to laugh and shout, with huge rolling eyes and long white teeth, and the donkey took fright. It ran and ran as fast as it could, every now and again bucking right up in the air, lashing out with its back legs. Abdulla held on to the rope round the donkey's neck very tightly with one hand, while he clutched his talisman with the other. When the Demon was left far behind. Abdulla got down off the donkey's back and spoke soothingly to it, and gave it a piece of carrot which he had in his pocket. So after a little while, they went on again.

By now it was nearly midday and was getting very hot, so Abdulla saw with joy the minarets of a mosque, and then the red stone wall of the caravan-serai.

'Seek out the Green-turbanned Doctor' advised the voice of the Good Peri. 'He is sitting in the teahouse, inside the middle gate.'

So Abdulla tied up the donkey near a water trough, and entered the teahouse, where all the men sat around in a circle drinking the hot liquid out of small bowls.

'Greetings, brother,' said the owner of the

teahouse, handing him a bowl of scalding hot tea, flavoured with cardamom, which he had filled up with water at the bubbling samovar. 'Have you come far?'

'Far enough, but this delicious tea will refresh me', said Abdulla, gratefully drinking, and eating some delicious meat pastry which the man put before him. All the other men were smoking pipes and talking together, and Abdulla looked about him as he ate and drank. After he had paid his bill, he became aware of a large bearded man with a green turban staring at him from across the room. He had a kind face, and the Good Peri said in Abdulla's ear:

'Go and speak to him, he is the one you seek.'

So Abdulla got up and made his way over to the Green-turbanned Doctor, who indicated a seat beside him on the low divan.

'My son,' said he, 'I know of your mission. Suffice it to say that you should take care, and wear this enchanted tunic on top of your clothes when you enter the certain part of the Blue Lake of Bundi-Amir, where you have to go for your certain task.'

'Good Doctor,' responded Abdulla, 'I thank you indeed for your kindness. But how am I to get to that certain part of the lake which you mention?"

The Green-turbanned Doctor put a finger to his lips. 'Not so loud, everything must be done with the utmost secrecy, I beg you. Now, have a rest here and feed your donkey, then leave at nightfall by the Eastern Gate of this caravanserai, where you will meet an aged Dervish. Listen to what he tells you, and carry on from there. Peace upon you, and Allah bless you!' So saying, the Green-turbanned Doctor got up and went his way.

The tunic which he had handed Abdulla was made of green fabric, with a bright iridescent sheen upon it, so Abdulla put it on top of his clothes and went to see about the donkey's food.

Just before nightfall, rested and fed, both Abdulla and his donkey left by the Eastern Gate as the Doctor had said they should. At the side of the road sat a very old, dreamy-eyed Dervish with a tattered robe and staff, just as Abdulla expected.

'This is the one from whom you will get further instructions,' said the voice of the Good Peri in his ear, and as it finished speaking Abdulla's eyes met those of the Dervish.

'Welcome, my son,' said he, 'Your purpose is known to me. Go on from here until you reach a large valley; there is a rest-house there in a small town, where you will meet a sailor with one eye. Go to him, and he will take you to the spot where you must jump into the Blue Lake of Bundi-Amir. Tell him to remain until you come to the surface once more, for he must bring you back safely to the valley. Go, and Peace and Blessings of Allah be upon you!' said he kindly. When Abdulla tried to thank him, the old Dervish had closed his eyes, and seemed to be sleeping.

So it came to pass that Abdulla and his donkey reached the valley, and in the noisy, colourful market-place he saw a dark-skinned sailor with one eye standing drinking from a horn cup.

'Speak to him,' said the voice of the Good Peri, 'for here is he whom you seek.'

Abdulla approached the sailor and said:

'I have come from the lady who has become a Fig-Pecker. Can you take me to that certain part of the lake where I have to descend in order to get the jar of perfume to enable her to regain her human shape?'

'Certainly, young sir,' replied the sailor instantly, 'Come with me and we shall set out at once.'

Thereupon he whistled, and a donkey appeared, which he mounted. Then, side by side, the dark, one-eyed sailor and Abdulla rode away.

When they finally arrived at the Blue Lake, the sailor pointed out where Abdulla should descend into the depths. The sailor lowered Abdulla on a long rope from the side of a small boat. The blue waters of Lake Bundi-Amir were as still as death.

'Abdulla, you are nearly there. Hold on to your talisman and wish sincerely for success,' said the voice of the Good Peri in his ear, 'because there will be many Deevs and monsters between you and the jar of perfume which you must bring up from the deep blue lake.'

No sooner had the waters closed over his head than Abdulla began to see all manner of Deevs, Afrits, and monsters below, swimming around him. He hung on to his talisman and after a little while the creatures fled away from him.

Soon he found himself at the very bottom of the lake and lo and behold! there was a huge cavern open before him. He could see the entrance quite clearly, and went on boldly, until he found himself right inside a vast underwater cave, with the walls gleaming with mother-of-pearl, and the floor studded with coral and precious gems. Dazzled by the sight, he looked around him. There was no one there, but the voice of the Good Peri urged him on.

'Go on a little further into the cave, Abdulla, go on until you see the jar of Perfume in a niche in the rocky wall.'

Sure enough, there he saw a minute later a small jar, standing in a niche, covered with tendrils of seaweed and hung around with strings of pearls.

'How can I touch it, Good Peri?' cried Abdulla, 'It looks as if it would not move to my fingers, it looks as if it ... it has been there a thousand years!'

'It has,' responded the voice of the Good Peri. 'Take it down and it will be quite easy to bring to the surface. Hurry, for the water will soon be very cold, and the magician who lives in the cavern may return...'

Quickly Abdulla grabbed the precious jar, pulling it away from the clinging weed and letting the strings of pearls fall to the coral floor. He gave a tug on the rope and the jaunty one-eyed sailor pulled him up to safety. They got to the shore in the small boat, and Abdulla changed out of his wet clothes.

'We must get back as quickly as possible,' said the sailor then, helping Abdulla to dress. The jar of Enchanted Perfume was gleaming like gold in the sun. Abdulla could see the miniature horse's heads on it clearly. 'Hide that in your cloak, for we must not let it be seen.' They went back the way they had come, on two donkeys.

A storm sprang up, the wild wind howled and the terrible lightning flashed. Abdulla was afraid that they would be struck by thunderbolts, for he had never seen such a storm in all his life. However, to cut a long story short, at last Abdulla was standing at the door of the walled house once more, with the precious jar hidden in the folds of his cloak.

The Lady's servant, on seeing Abdulla, at once led him to the room where the Fig-Pecker was still on the silver perch in the window.

'Hurry, hurry, let me have the flask of Enchanted Perfume poured over my head,' pleaded the bird with flapping wings, 'Release me from this odious shape or I shall die.'

'Patience, dear Mistress,' crooned the old woman, struggling with the top of the flask, while Abdulla looked on with much interest.

In a few moments the cork flew out and the sweet scented liquid was poured over the small brown bird's head. There was a great clap of thunder, smoke poured into the room, and everything went black. Abdulla saw flames consume the body of the bird, and it was soon reduced to ashes. The old woman began to weep and to beat her breast, crying,

'My mistress, my mistress, what in the name of Allah has happened? Alas, alas, she is reduced to ashes, O! shall I ever see her again?'

'Have no fear,' came a voice from the small pile of ashes on the floor, 'Look, I am restored to my own form once more, thanks to the efforts of this noble young man.'

A tall, slim, veiled figure, dressed in silks and jewels, as radiant as the sun, advanced towards them from the spot where the ashes lay. The room cleared of smoke and the light of day streamed into the room. The servant cried now for joy, tears pouring down her cheeks at seeing her beloved mistress restored to human shape.

Abdulla could scarcely believe his eyes, and fell to his knees in front of the splendid lady.

'No, do not kneel to me,' said she, putting out her hand, 'Come now to my treasure chests, and I will pay you for your efforts on my behalf.'

She led the way to a cellar which was stacked from floor to ceiling with magnificent chests of chased silver, filled with gold coins. The Lady bade her servant fill a bag with gold and then handed it to Abdulla.

'Take these, they will last you the rest of your days,' she said sweetly. 'As soon as the bag empties, it will again be filled by magical means. Peace be upon you, go your way. I shall always be grateful.'

Before Abdulla could thank her she was gone.

The old woman took him back up the stairs and into the street, and thanked him with all her might and main, telling him that he was the bravest creature on Earth.

The bag of gold coins was soon hidden in his cloak, and Abdulla found his donkey outside the gate, brought by the dark-skinned one-eyed sailor while he was in the house. So Abdulla returned in great triumph to his home, and told his mother of his good fortune.

When they had entertained all their friends for seven days and nights, Abdulla caused a fine house to be built for his mother. There she lived in peace and prosperity, for the gold in the bag never came to an end. Abdulla became a merchant, and travelled from Afghanistan to India, Khorassan to Tus. But never again did he see the jaunty one-eyed sailor, the Green-turbanned Doctor, or the tattered dreamy old Dervish.

The enchanted lady who had been turned into a Fig-Pecker married a handsome foreign prince and went to his country to live in great happiness. So when next he came into Kabul and saw the great noble house empty, Abdulla bought it and lived there. The Good Peri remained with him for the rest of his days, telling him what to do and say. And often, when he was a revered old man, gathering his children and grandchildren around him, he told them the story of the Lady who became a Fig-Pecker, and how he saved her with the magic perfume from the bottom of the Blue Lake of Bundi-Amir.

The Well-Digger and the Deev

Once upon a time there was a strong young man called Yusuf who was a well-digger, and he was sent by the head-man of the village of Kamdeh to look at a well which had apparently run dry. The villagers had not been able to get water for days, for it had become blocked by some obstacle. The well was at the foot of the mountain, and it was thought a falling rock had rolled into it.

Yusuf let himself down into the well on the end of a rope, with his spade tied to his back. It was very dark at the bottom and he could see nothing. Then he took his spade, probed hither and thither, and struck something hard at last.

'Aha!' thought Yusuf to himself, 'This is the obstacle. But whatever can it be, it does not seem to be a rock? It might perhaps be a cow which has fallen in.'

Still there was no sign of water, and Yusuf started banging with his spade at the object at the bottom of the well. There was a loud cry, as of a demon in pain, and Yusuf, whose eyes were becoming used to the dark, saw he was standing on the head of a gigantic Deev, whose teeth were gleaming white, and whose eyes were rolling in agony.

'Human wretch!' bellowed the Deev, 'Stop hacking at me with that instrument. What are you doing here?'

'I am a well-digger, honourable Deev', replied Yusuf, 'and the head-man of the village has just sent me down to see what was blocking the well, for the people cannot get any water.'

'Why should they get water? I want it to stand in to cool my feet,' snapped the Deev, 'and if you do not promise to do everything I ask, I shall drop you into the water and drown you.'

Yusuf promised to do whatever the Deev should require, for he had no other choice if he wanted to live.

'Bring me a cart-load of grapes, I intend to stay down here,' said the Deev. 'Go back to the village, bring me the grapes, and drop them into the well for me to eat.'

'Certainly, I will go at once,' said Yusuf, and climbed up the rope back into the sunlight.

When he got to the head-man's house he told him:

'Sir, I have found out what is wrong with the well and why the people cannot get any water. There is a Deev living in it, and I only escaped with my life by promising to do exactly what the horrible creature says.'

'Allah have mercy upon us!' cried the head-man, 'Why, what does it want?'

'A cart-load of grapes,' replied Yusuf, and soon he and all the other villagers were collecting grapes from the best vines to put into a cart for the Deev.

By the time Yusuf got back to the well, the Deev was looking out, with its large red-rimmed eyes ablaze.

'Where have you been, wretched human?' it greeted him, 'I have become so impatient I think I will tear you limb from limb!'

'No, no, do not do that,' pleaded Yusuf, 'for who will bring you the things you need if you destroy me? The villagers are terrified and would not come near you.'

'Oh, very well then,' grumbled the Deev, 'Toss the grapes down, and be quick about it.'

Soon the cart was empty and Yusuf asked:

'Is there anything more you want? I shall come back tomorrow, if you wish.'

'Yes, tomorrow bring me a cartful of dates,' said the Deev, 'and if you do not come I shall have to go to the village and collect them myself.'

'No, no, don't do that, I will bring them,' said Yusuf.

'All right,' grunted the Deev, chewing up bunches of grapes. 'But be sure you do, or I shall come out.'

The people of the village began to weep and wail when they heard what had happened, for not only was their water supply cut off, but they would soon lose their fruit if they had to send it all to the Deev.

That night there was a meeting at the head-man's house, and everyone was asked to speak if they had any ideas for getting rid of the Deev. Tempers ran high, for the three oldest men in the village always quarrelled on these occasions. But although they talked for hours, nobody could think of any plan which would be effective enough.

Next day Yusuf was sent with the cart-load of dates, and the Deev was waiting for him most impatiently.

'Where have you been?' grumbled the Deev, with outstretched claws as Yusuf approached with the first sack of dates, 'Hurry, for I am so hungry that I shall eat you as soon as look at you this morning!'

'Oh, do not do that,' said Yusuf, 'for no one else would bring you anything at all.'

'Very well,' said the Deev ungraciously, 'But be sure and bring a cart-load of sweetmeats next time, the finest hulwa that can be made, for I desire it. Go on, back to the village, and get every person to make some, for I shall require a full cart-load first thing tomorrow morning.'

When Yusuf got back home the villagers crowded round him and he told them the Deev had demanded hulwa. But they wailed and shouted.

'What are we going to do about water, for our families are crying for something to drink, and our clothes are all dirty for want of washing?'

And Yusuf answered:

'Good friends, we must have patience, for a Deev the size of the one I have seen at the bottom of the well cannot be moved like a bag of cats.'

Then they went back to their homes and milked their goats to give the children a drink, and began to make hulwa.

Just at midday, as Yusuf was buying a watermelon to take home to his wife, a very old man in a patched Dervish's cloak came up to him.

'My son,' said the Dervish, 'I hear that there is a Deev in the village well. I think I know what to do to get rid of it. But first, you must obey my orders.'

'Most excellent Dervish,' cried the well-digger, 'I am entirely at your command, ask me anything, and I shall do it.'

'First,' said the Dervish, 'Pick seven leaves from yonder tree, and seven sprigs of wild thyme. Burn those together until they are ashes, and make those ashes into a powder.'

So Yusuf did as he was told, and returned with the powder in a corner of his handkerchief.

'Now, when the villagers have made the hulwa, sprinkle this powder on it, whispering the name of Suliman, Son of David (on whom be Peace) and feed it to the Deev.' So saying, the Dervish walked away, before Yusuf could ask him what was likely to happen.

When the head-man of the village went round from house to house with several men collecting the hulwa, Yusuf sprinkled the powder on to each piece, whispering 'In the name of Suliman, Son of David, (on whom be Peace)'. Soon the cart was full, and Yusuf went off with it.

This time the Deev was hungrier than ever, and its eyes were redder than Yusuf had seen them before.

'Hurry up, insignificant human,' shouted the Deev, furiously clawing at the top of the well, 'What have you been doing all this time? I was ready for the hulwa hours ago.'

'One special ingredient had to be added at the last moment,' said Yusuf truthfully, and handed down the first tray of sweetmeats. One lot after another vanished and at last there were none left.

'Tomorrow you must bring me two cart-loads of the finest melons you can find,' came the voice of the Deev from the bottom of the well, where it stood, gorged and sleepy, with its feet in the cool, fresh water.

Yusuf was just about to reply, when to his great surprise the Deev began to swell and swell until it seemed about to burst. Its head came up out of the well, growing larger every minute, and then the rest of its body, swelling up like a gigantic inflated water-skin. For a few seconds it hovered above the well, water dripping from its huge clawed feet, then, with a blood-curdling moan, flew up into the sky, bobbing about as if it were an enormous balloon. Yusuf strained his eyes to catch a last glimpse as it disappeared into the clouds. There was at that moment a loud bang, as of the loudest clap of thunder, and Yusuf ran back to the village as fast as his legs would carry him to tell what had happened.

At first the villagers were terrified to go to collect water in case the dreadful creature came back. But the head-man soothed their fears, for the Dervish had told him before he continued on his wanderings that this was what would happen when the magic powder, which was sprinkled on the hulwa, began to act.

So young and old went off to the well with water-skins and earthenware pots, laughing with joy. They roasted a whole sheep that night and gave Yusuf a great feast in honour of his courage in dealing with the fearful Deev.

And Yusuf dug many wells all over the God-gifted Kingdom of Afghanistan, because his name had become famous throughout the land.

The King's Favourite and the Beautiful Slave

Once upon a time there was a good King, who had at his Court a favourite courtier, whom he loved as if he were a brother.

This courtier, one Abdul by name, was tall and handsome, witty and beloved by all. His special position at Court made it possible for him to play the flute to the ladies of the harem, and he fell deeply in love with one of them. This was the beautiful Roshana, a slave of the Queen. She was as sweet as she was lovely, and when she saw that Abdul looked on her with approval, she was highly delighted.

One day a messenger arrived from Abdul bringing his proposal of marriage, and with great joy she sent back her answer. She replied that nothing in the world would make her more happy, if they could get the Queen's permission and blessing.

Abdul went at once to the King and told him the whole story.

'Your Majesty,' said he, 'If I cannot have this beautiful slave to be my wife I shall die. I have never felt like this in all my life.'

The King smiled. 'Abdul, be at peace,' he said kindly, 'I shall arrange this affair. Roshana shall be yours as soon as I can speak to the Queen to release her from her duties.'

He was as good as his word. Next day, with the blessings of the royal family, the happy pair were united in marriage with the greatest pomp and splendour.

The ruler gave them a wonderful feast in honour of

the occasion, and a bag of gold which should have lasted them for years. However, being so fond of fine sweetmeats and pastries, they spent a great deal of money giving parties to their friends, and their money began to go very fast. Life at the Royal Court had accustomed them to high living, and also they had a wide circle of acquaintances in all walks of society.

When twelve months had passed, the bag of gold which the monarch had given them was empty. There were a lot of creditors to be paid, the tailor, the jeweller, the dressmaker, the shoemaker, and the pastry shop. So they sold all their wedding presents, and paid their bills. When that was done they only had the clothes they stood up in.

'Wife,' said Abdul, 'There is no doubt about it, we shall have to get some money from somewhere. The salary which I get at Court is not nearly enough for us to live upon, with our expensive tastes. What shall we do?'

'Ask the King for some more, of course,' said Roshana, 'and I shall ask the Queen...'

'No, no, my love, we cannot do that, we have spent so much they will be most annoyed. Let us think of a plan.' And Abdul buried his head in his hands. Suddenly he cried:

'I know, I have it. We will pretend to die.'

'Why,' said Roshana, 'How can we do that, and for what reason?'

'Listen,' said the King's favourite, 'You shall put ashes on your head and go to the King telling him that *I* have died, and he will give you something.'

Then they both went to the oven and sprinkled each other's heads with ashes. First, Roshana, in mourning clothes, presented herself at the Queen's apartments.

'My Lady Queen,' she cried, 'The most dreadful thing has happened.... Alas, alas, poor Abdul is dead, and I have not any money left in the world even to bury him.'

Then the Queen was very sorry for her and caused the sum of one thousand gold-pieces to be given to the girl. Also she gave a piece of pure white linen, so that Roshana could wrap up her husband's body suitably for burial.

Roshana was delighted, and thanked her royal mistress with all her heart. She went back home, stuffing her veil into her mouth to stop from laughing, and told her husband what had happened.

'Look, here are a thousand pieces of gold for us to spend!' she said. 'You go to the King and see what you can get.'

When Abdul stood before the King in his mourning clothes and with ashes on his head his royal master was most sympathetic.

'My poor man,' said he, 'What is the matter with you?'

'Imperial Majesty, Great King,' moaned the favourite, 'My wife is dead, and I have no money left in the world with which to bury her. Alas, alas, in a year we have spent the generous allowance your majesty gave us as a wedding present.'

'Grieve no more, unhappy Abdul,' said the King. 'Here are two thousand gold-pieces: take them, go and arrange your wife's funeral. Also take one of the finest pieces of white linen that there is in the Palace and use it for a winding-sheet.'

When Abdul got back home, covering his face with his handkerchief to stifle his laughter, he handed over the money to Roshana.

'See, I have got twice as much as you did,' said he, 'What a good thing it is to be the King's favourite.' Then they sat happily counting the coins into a wooden chest.

Now the Queen, who had a good heart, went to the monarch's apartment to console him.

'Your Majesty,' said she, 'I am sorry to hear of the death of your favourite, may Allah have mercy on his soul!'

'Wife, are you mad?' cried the King, 'It is not my good Abdul who has died, it is your slave-girl Roshana, for he was at Court this very morning with ashes on his head, telling me all about it.'

'No, no, you are mistaken,' she said, 'For it was Roshana who came to me in her mourning clothes, and with ashes on her head, not an hour ago, to tell me about her husband's sudden death.'

Then they started to argue so loudly that they were overheard by the Grand Vizir, who entered the room with a discreet cough.

'Imperial Majesty,' said he, 'Allow me to go to the house of this unfortunate pair to ascertain the true state of affairs. I shall go there and find out, by looking in at the window with my own eyes.'

So the King gave him permission to do what had been suggested, and the Grand Vizir went to Abdul's house.

Roshana, who had been looking out of the upstairs window from behind the curtain, saw the Grand Vizir's arrival, and only just in time she called out:

'Husband, husband, lie down and pretend to be dead, for the Grand Vizir is approaching!'

So quickly Abdul lay down on the bed and, holding his breath, covered himself with the white linen, from top to toe.

Sure enough, when the Grand Vizir looked through the window he saw Roshana in her mourning clothes, weeping and wailing, beating her breast and tearing her hair in grief. There on the bed lay the body of Abdul decently wrapped in finest linen, apparently quite dead.

The Grand Vizir returned to the Court and told the King that it was obvious that Abdul was dead.

'I saw with my own eyes,' said he, 'Roshana in grief

beating her breast and crying.'

The King looked at his wife and inclined his head.

'Of course I was right, my dear,' he said. 'Now go back to your own apartments, for the Grand Vizir has ascertained the truth of the matter to my satisfaction.'

'But not to mine!' cried the Queen in a rage, 'For I think that it is the other way round, and I shall make it my business to find out.'

She called her oldest and most trusted slave-woman to her side and gave her instructions to go and have a look on her royal mistress's behalf. For the Queen believed that she was right and the King was wrong.

The old woman set off and arrived at Abdul's house. As luck would have it, the favourite was looking out of the window, and shouted to Roshana:

'Wife, wife, get into bed and cover yourself with the linen sheet, for the Queen's slave-woman is coming, and she must see you apparently dead!'

So quickly Roshana lay down, and when the old woman applied her eye to the keyhole, there was Abdul moaning over the body of Roshana. The servant went back to the Palace and informed her royal mistress that she had seen with her own eyes the bereaved husband, and Roshana obviously dead.

When the Queen heard this she got into a state of excitement, and resolved to speak to the King again.

'Your Majesty,' she said, 'My most trusted slave-woman has just reported to me that it is truly Roshana who is dead!'

'Upon my soul!' shouted the infuriated monarch, 'I shall go and see for myself!'

'So shall I!' insisted the Queen, and so the whole royal party, courtiers, servants and all, arrived outside the house.

Seeing the people in the garden, Abdul and Roshana both lay down, side by side, covering themselves with the linen and keeping absolutely still.

The Grand Vizir opened the door, and both King and Queen stood looking at the bodies on the bed.

'There, now they are both dead,' said the King, finally.

'But my slave-girl died afterwards, obviously,' said the Queen.

'No, no,' said the King, 'Poor Abdul must have died last, for he came to me to tell me about his wife's death. I wish that someone could tell me the way things went, it is a great mystery.' Then, turning to his Grand Vizir, he added, 'I would give a thousand pieces of gold to anyone who could tell me exactly who died first!'

Unable to control himself, Abdul then threw off the linen and cried:

'Give me the money, O Fountain of Wisdom, for I will tell you. *I* died first!'

At that moment Roshana threw off her shroud and cried:

'Give me the money, for I will tell you!' Then, overcome with laughter, she sank on the floor at the King's feet. Soon the King and the Queen were both laughing too, and thought it was a great joke. Also they were both so pleased that their favourites were still alive, that they forgave them everything and gave them another large bag of gold which lasted many years. And Allah lengthened all their days.

The Princess and the Bulbul

Once upon a time there lived a Princess, called Ayesha, who had a pet bulbul. Now a bulbul is a nightingale, which sings all night long, and Ayesha loved hers dearly.

One night when the moon was full and the restless Princess Ayesha could not sleep, she got up and went to the bird's cage and said to it:

'Will you sing me a song that will put me to sleep, for I want to dream again of a strange country that appears sometimes to me when I have gone to sleep?'

And the bulbul answered:

'I cannot sing tonight, Mistress, for my heart is sore, but if you will take me out of my cage I will tell you my story.'

Princess Ayesha was intrigued at the bird's words, for she did not know that it could speak in the language of humans, so she opened the door of the carved ivory cage and the nightingale hopped out and sat on her hand.

'Know, O Princess,' began the creature, 'that I am not a bird but the son of a king, who was stolen away from my father's palace by a wicked Deev and turned into a bird until such time as I can be rescued.'

'What a strange thing it must be to be bewitched!' cried the Princess, 'How does it feel?'

'Well, it is not pleasant to be a bird in a cage and have to sing all night,' replied the bulbul. 'But I must put up with the situation until the magic powder to turn me back into a prince is found.'

'And how is that to be done?' said the Princess, for

she was most interested as to what the nightingale would look like in his human form.

'I will tell you,' replied the bulbul. 'You know the strange country which appears to you sometimes when you are asleep?'

'Yes,' said she, 'It is a beautiful place, with great tall trees and running rivers full of fish, golden boats with golden sails, and a castle with towering turrets.'

'Well,' the bird explained, 'That is the Land of Enchantment, where a Giant Deev keeps a sack of the magic powder which turns humans back into their original shape if transformed into any other form by magical means.'

'Then how can I help you,' asked the Princess, 'to get some of this powder? Tell me where I can find the Giant Deev and I will go there and bring some of it back.'

'I will sing you to sleep, and when you get to the Enchanted Land, you must follow the river until you come to the bridge. Cross the bridge and pass over to the other side. Soon you will see a great red-stone castle, with a very beautiful garden all around it. Go through the tree-lined walk, through the small glass door which leads from the garden into the Giant's bedroom, and you will find the sack of powder under his bed.'

'Oh, bulbul, quickly sing me to sleep and I will be away to the Enchanted Land as soon as my eyes close,' said Ayesha.

'One word of warning, do not eat or drink anything while you are there, for if you do so you will never wake, and I shall be doomed to live on the face of the Earth as a bird for the rest of my days,' said the nightingale. 'And you will never return home, alas.'

Then Ayesha lay back on her bed, and the bird began to sing, and in a few moments her eyes closed and she was in a dream. The nightingale hopped back into the ivory cage and closed the door to wait until the Princess should wake.

Now, no sooner had Ayesha arrived in the Enchanted Land than she began to walk as quickly as she could towards the river. When she reached it she stopped to gaze in wonder at the beautiful coloured fish which were swimming about in the clear water. She was just going to sit down on the river bank and rest when a purple and green fish popped out of the water and said:

'Princess, Princess, do not stay, you must go on and cross the bridge to the Giant Deev's castle. For if you do not take back the magic powder quickly, the poor bulbul will die.'

'How do you know about the nightingale?' cried the Princess in astonishment.

'Ah, we are all magical creatures here in this land of Enchantment,' said the purple and green fish, and jumping back into the water it swam out of sight.

Ayesha started walking again, and soon she was over the river on the other side. She was just going to sit down on the river bank, when a turquoise bird swooped down from a tree and said to her:

'Hurry on Princess, go quickly to the Giant Deev's castle, for if you do not get back quickly with the magic powder, the poor bird will die.'

'How do you know?' cried the Princess in surprise.

'Because we are all enchanted creatures, of course,' said the turquoise bird, and flew away.

After she had walked for a long time, Ayesha saw the turrets of a huge castle in front of her. There did not seem to be anyone about, so she was able to go quite easily into the flowery garden and up the tree-lined walk. Through the garden she went, and though she saw beautiful fruits hanging from the branches of the trees she recalled the words of the bulbul. She knew she must not eat or drink anything or she would never return home, and that the bird would be sure to die.

So, hungry and thirsty, and with aching feet, she went slowly through the garden, looking for the glass door which led into the Giant Deev's bedroom.

Suddenly, she saw it, and quietly turned the silver door-knob. Inside the room there was a very large bed, with a feather quilt upon it, and under the bed Ayesha could see a sack. This was the sack which contained the magic powder. She wriggled under the bed, and managed to open the mouth of the sack, and took out a pinch of the white powder. She had just tied the powder into a corner of her silken handkerchief, when she heard a tremendous noise. It was the Giant Deev returning. The ground shook, and the windows rattled, and Ayesha felt her heart was in her mouth. Should she run or stay under the bed? Suddenly the Giant Deev was in the room, and threw himself down on the bed. Then Ayesha felt the springs quiver and the floor shake as the Giant Deev began to snore. Under the bed, with the precious powder safely in her handkerchief, Ayesha breathed a sigh of relief. She crawled on hands and knees, and crept through the glass door, and out into the garden. A huge hairy dog with large white teeth sprang at her as she ran through the trees, but she ran and ran until she reached the gate, when the dog gave up chasing her. Up the road to the bridge she hurried, stumbling and falling, with dry lips, longing for a drink of water. When she got to the river she bent down and was just about to take a drink, when the purple and green fish jumped up in the air and said:

'Don't drink, don't drink. Remember ... remember.... If you do you will never leave the Enchanted Land, and the bulbul who is a Prince will die.'

And so she stopped just in time, and ran until she

reached the very spot where she had first opened her eyes in the Land of Enchantment long ago. Her feet hurt terribly and her slippers were torn on the sharp stones, but still she ran on, until she fell and could not get up, and a blackness seemed to come in front of her eyes.

When she regained consciousness she was back in her own bed, with dry mouth and aching head. In her hand was her handkerchief with the magic powder tied up in one corner in a knot. She jumped to her feet and whispered to the bird in his ivory cage:

'Bulbul, bulbul, look what I have got! I have been to the Land of Enchantment and have brought back the magic powder.'

As she spoke, the nightingale fluttered from the cage and came to sit upon her hand. Ayesha sprinkled the pinch of white powder on the bird's head, and in a trice there was a tall, handsome young man standing there beside her, dressed in an embroidered robe.

Ayesha was so surprised that she fainted away.

When she came to herself, she was being given a glass of water by her devoted old nurse, and the fine young man was rubbing her hands with rose-water that a slave-boy was pouring into a crystal bowl.

'Where am I?' asked the Princess faintly, then she remembered everything.

'Your Highness, thank you a thousand times for going to get the magic powder for me from the Land of Enchantment,' said the Prince. 'If you will accept me, I should like to marry you at once and take you as my wife to my own land.'

Ayesha joyfully agreed, and her father the King gave the young pair his blessing. So they went away to the Prince's country and lived happily ever afterwards. And Allah sent them many sons.

But never again, no matter how hard she tried,

could the Princess Ayesha dream of that strange and marvellous magic Land of Enchantment. Where it was, and how far is the journey, we shall never know.

The Magic Shawl and the Enchanted Trumpet

Once upon a time, long ago, three soldiers who had served together in all the battles of Tamerlane, Timur-i-Lang, decided to join forces and go back to their home village together. They travelled for a long time, hoping that soon they might see their families again.

Reaching a dark, gloomy mountain pass, they decided to rest until morning and find the best way round the mountain in the light of day. So two of them lay down to sleep in the shelter of a rock, while the third, one Feroz by name, kept watch so that no wild animals or thieves could attack them while they slept. The moon rose high in the sky, the owls hooted, and Feroz warmed himself beside the fire he had lit with pieces of dry wood. He had not sat there very long when suddenly there came, as if from nowhere, a tattered Dervish, who said, 'Peace be upon you, my son. What are you doing here?'

And Feroz answered, 'I am a soldier returning home from the wars. There are my two companions of many battles, sleeping, while I keep watch.'

'May I sit down with you for a little while and warm myself beside your fire?' asked the Dervish.

'Certainly, please do', replied the other, and they sat together until the clouds hid the moon.

'Have you any family?' asked the Dervish, stretching out his hands to the fire.

'Only my old mother and father, who were very poor indeed when I enlisted in the ranks,' said Feroz. 'Now, returning as I am, empty handed, I fear that I may be a burden to them. But I should like to see them before they die, all the same.'

'Take this shawl,' said the Dervish, pulling a piece of brown woollen material from his bundle. 'If you put it on your shoulders and wish, you may have anything you desire. But never tell a woman the secret of the shawl. Remember this, or it will be the worse for you.'

Feroz thanked the Dervish very much and put it in his leather pouch. Then as the dawn was breaking he gave the old man a cup of tea, and roused his friends from their sleep. When he turned round to speak to the Dervish he found that the ancient had vanished. So Feroz told the others about the magic shawl, and put it round his shoulders to wish for some gold. The other two would not believe such a tale and laughed, saying, 'Brother, you must have been having a wonderful dream.'

Just as they began drinking their tea, there was a tinkling sound, and to their great surprise, a small pile of gold coins appeared on the ground in front of Feroz.

'Haha, you see, friends, this *is* a magic wishing shawl, and the Dervish was right; I only have to wish, with the shawl around my shoulders, and it is done.'

'Wish for some gold for us, brother, please,' cried the others, and he did, and it was not long before a pile of gold coins appeared in front of each of them.

So, they forgot all about going to see their old fathers and mothers, and travelled about the country in great style, with gold to spend on every delicacy that could be bought. They were dressed in fine clothes, had plenty to eat, and never lacked for anything. And they prayed to Allah to lengthen their days.

But after a time they grew tired of travelling and Feroz decided to have a fine castle. He put on the wishing shawl and cried; 'I wish for a castle where we may all live in splendour.'

In a few moments it stood before their eyes, with great towering turrets, high walls with guards looking out in all directions, and beautiful gardens full of flowers. And out of the gate came three grooms, with three fine Arabian steeds, saddled and bridled, to take them riding.

This was very well for a time, but they found that it was not very interesting to stay at home for always. So one day they filled their saddle-bags with jewels, precious silks, and flasks of priceless scent, and went to visit the king of the neighbouring country.

Now, this king had an only daughter, as beautiful as the day, and when she looked out of her window and saw the three young men so splendidly dressed, arriving in her father's courtyard, she thought they must surely be kings' sons; so, veiling herself, she came to the Hall of Audience to watch when her father greeted them.

The king was very pleased at the gifts they brought, the precious stones, rare silks and scents, and he gave a great feast, lasting seven days and seven nights. Roast camels stuffed with sheep were served, and the sheep were stuffed with peacocks, and the peacocks were stuffed with herbs, and the whole week passed in jollity.

Now, the Princess was interested in the shawl that Feroz was wearing over his shoulders, and asked him about its origin. For a moment he thought he had better not tell her the truth, but after she prettily asked him again he gave in.

'Lady,' said he, 'this is a magic wishing shawl, which was given to me by an old Dervish when I was a poor soldier. I have only to think of something whilst I have it around my shoulders, and my wish is granted.'

'Oh,' cried the Princess, 'Could you wish for a golden bracelet for me, set with the blood-red rubies of Badakshan?' She wanted to test him and to see for herself if this were true.

'Certainly,' said Feroz, and when he had asked for it the bracelet appeared on the Princess's arm. Now, being very cunning and artful, and wanting to have the magic shawl for her own, the Princess went away and made a shawl so like the enchanted one that they could not be told apart. Then, that night she crept into the room where Feroz was sleeping and stole his shawl, leaving the other in its place,

In the morning the three friends came to pay their respects to the King and request his permission to go on their way, for they wished to return to their castle. He gave them his blessing, and they rode away.

Soon after they arrived back Feroz, needing some money, put on the shawl and wished. Nothing happened. He tried again, and still nothing happened. Yet a third time he tried; then he examined the shawl, and realized that his had been exchanged for another. He sorrowfully remembered telling the Princess about the magic properties of the shawl.

The other two friends were very upset indeed about this, for their fine extravagant life was now at an end. It seemed impossible that they could live again in the impoverished way they did when they had first met the old Dervish.

So Feroz hit upon a plan, and it was this: that he should go in disguise to the King's Palace, gain admittance to the Harem, and steal back the shawl from the Princess.

As Feroz put on an old cloak and trudged out of the gate, he found that the Dervish was walking beside him.

'Good morning, my son,' said the old man, 'And

what has happened to you since we last met?'

'Alas, father,' said Feroz, 'I have lost the magic shawl which you so kindly gave me, and now I am forced to go out and try to seek it in the Harem of the King, for his daughter stole it while I was a guest of her father. I forgot your advice, and told her.'

'Take this trumpet, it belonged to Iskandar the Great,' said the Dervish, 'and when you blow a blast upon it, a troop of horsemen shall come to your aid. When you get to the Palace of the king do not try to get into the Harem, for the king's Eunuchs will assuredly strike off your head if you are found, but blow the trumpet instead, and see what happens.' He thrust an ancient trumpet into Feroz's hand. Before the astonished Feroz could thank him, the Dervish had vanished.

Then Feroz went back to the castle and told his friends about the timely visit of the miraculous Dervish. He put the trumpet to his lips and played a military tune upon it, loud and long. Before he had finished, the whole courtyard of the castle was full of soldiers on horseback, and the air resounded with the neighing of gallant steeds.

With his friends on either side, Feroz began to lead the troops out to make war upon the army of the King. When the King's palace was besieged, Feroz called to him, 'Let your daughter return to us the magic shawl which she has stolen, and we shall go away in peace.'

The King went to his daughter's room and tried to reason with her to give the shawl back. But she said, 'Father, let us try if I can beat them one way or another, for the shawl which gives everything for which one can wish is a rare treasure indeed. Tell them I will hand it to them tomorrow at noon.' But she had a plan to steal the fantastic trumpet, for she had heard about its magical powers.

So the King sent his Grand Vizir to ask the besiegers to wait until noon next day, when he promised his daughter would hand over the shawl.

Now, dressing herself in a servant's clothing, the Princess went out of the Palace at night with a basket on her arm, full of delicious fruits and sweets, and veiled, she sang to the soldiers as they sat round the bonfires beneath the Palace walls. Hither and thither she went, until she came to the tent where Feroz lay sleeping. There, on the tent-pole, hung the magic trumpet, which could summon an army at one blast. She took it quietly, put it into her basket, and slipped back the way she had come. Then she went to her father the King and said, 'Look, I have the secret of Feroz's power. This is an enchanted trumpet. Blow it, O my Father, and all the troops of our besieger will be in our fortress and not outside, attacking us. For this is the trumpet of Iskandar the Great and the troops of cavalry come at one long blow.'

The King put the trumpet to his lips and blew a great blast, and all the men on horseback who had been outside the Palace suddenly appeared inside the fortress ready to fight for him.

So Feroz and his friends were once more penniless and alone, without an army or protection, as forlorn as they were when the Dervish first came to Feroz at the foot of the mountains that night long ago.

Now the three soldiers began to walk away homewards again, for they thought that what had happened must have been only a dream which they had dreamt together. They struggled on until they came to a wood, and there they lay down to rest. When his two friends had gone to sleep, Feroz sat wide, wide awake, for he thought he had better keep watch. And as he watched he began to feel lonely for his old home village and his parents.

Suddenly the ancient Dervish appeared again, and said as before, 'Peace be upon you, my son. What are you doing here?'

And Feroz answered, 'O Father of Wisdom, the magic shawl and the trumpet which you gave me are now gone, stolen by that wicked princess: but now we are weary of travelling and intrigues and want to see our fathers and mothers once more.'

The Dervish said, 'My son, you have learned that one cannot have everything which one wants by just wishing, and that even if one has the magic trumpet of Iskandar it can pass into other hands. I shall now give you something which will endure for the rest of your days, and which you should use for the good of others, as well as for yourself.'

'What is it, father?' cried Feroz as the Dervish drew forth from his bag an ancient hand woven saddle-bag with strange designs upon it.

'In this saddle-bag,' said the Dervish, 'is sufficient food for a meal. You may eat from it every day until you have reached your home, and then you will be able to do good to others by feeding anyone in need. It will neither be stolen from you, nor can it lose its magical properties, so use it well, my son, and blessings be upon you.' So saying, the Dervish vanished.

Feroz plunged his hand into the saddle-bag and took out enough food for his hunger to be satisfied. Then he woke his friends and they, too, ate their fill.

After three days they reached the village from which they had first set out to go and fight in the army of Timur-i-Lang. They found the thirty villagers were all suffering from famine and almost dead from hunger, for the crops had failed. So Feroz was able to go from house to house and feed everyone, while his two friends helped to bury those who had died.

Feroz embraced his old father and mother, and fed them with great care, for they were weak with hunger. Then he sat down and gave thanks to Allah that he should have been able to help so many of his own people. And the magic saddle-bag gave him all he needed for the rest of his days.

The Well of Everlasting Life

Once upon a time there lived a King who had one wish, and that was to live for ever. He had heard that far away, beyond the sands of Seistan, there was a well which had water of a clear crystal coldness, possessed of certain magic properties. People said that anyone who drank from this well would never die.

So, when his son Prince Daoud was old enough to know of his secret wish, the King said, 'Daoud my son, jewel of my eyes, go and bring me some of the water of the Well of Everlasting Life, for I would like to live for ever. And you too, you shall live for ever also, we shall become immortal.'

The Prince dressed himself for a journey, taking only robes such as pilgrims wear, and with a flask to fill with the magic water, he set out from the land of his birth.

He travelled and travelled away to the farthest part of the world. There he met an old hermit, a dervish, to whom he addressed himself respectfully.

'Honoured sir,' said he, 'Can you direct me to the Well of Everlasting Life? I have asked all along the way from the land of my birth and no one has known where it might be.'

'King's son,' replied the hermit, for all things were known to him and he could see through the Prince's disguise, 'The Well of Everlasting Life lies not more than half a mile from here, as the crow flies. It is inside a cave at the foot of these mountains,' and he pointed towards it with his staff.

'I thank you a thousand times, master,' said

Daoud, 'I am full of joy at having discovered it, for my father has sent me on this mission, and I have been away from the land of my birth a year and a day. Now I can take some of the water with me, so that he need never die.'

The old man looked at the young prince for a moment, then he said, 'When you go into the cave, heed the words of the wise bird which lives there.' Then he turned away and trudged off.

'Strange,' thought Daoud, 'What sort of bird would there be in the cave, and what would it say?'

Very soon he was standing inside the entrance of the cave. There was a strange glow at the other end of the cave, and Daoud went towards it. As his eyes became used to the gloom he saw that there was a well which seemed to go down, down, down, to the very bowels of the Earth, and Daoud felt quite dizzy as he looked into it. Trembling with excitement, he reached for the bucket and began to lower it into the well.

When the water came up from the depths it was crystal-clear and as cold as ice to the touch. Daoud said to himself, 'I will fill my father's flask and then take a drink of the magic water myself, so that I can benefit from the properties of this well, and become immortal myself.'

Just as he was about to place the flask inside the bucket he had drawn up, he heard a strange, shrill voice. It said, 'Stop, young man, do not take the Water of Everlasting Life until you have heard me speak.'

Amazed, the Prince looked about him, and saw a very ancient and draggle-tailed bird sitting on a perch in a shadowy nook. 'Look carefully at me. I was once a young bird, full of vigour and health, able to fly in the air, strong and free. Now, having drunk of the magic waters of this well, I am doomed to live here for ever, with dim eyes, lustreless feathers, and no joy left in life; all my one-time companions are dead, and the birds of the air will have nothing to do with me now, for I am not of their day or age.'

'Then the magic waters of this well only keep one alive, without renewing anything?' cried the Prince in horror.

'Yes, thus it is that you see me this way. Think, then, how it would be with you and anyone else who sips of this water. Look upon me as a terrible lesson. If I could only die and have peace, how happy I would be.' And the bird gave a deep sigh. 'But now I must live for ever like this.'

'So that was what the old Dervish meant when he asked me to be sure and heed the words of the bird in the cave,' Daoud said to himself. He leaned over the well, and quickly poured back into the depths the bucketful which he had drawn up.

He would go back to his father and explain, for it would be no pleasure to live on in the world, having no thoughts of Paradise upon which to dwell, but condemned to remain on earth for ever.

Thereupon he bade the aged bird goodbye and went back the way that he had come, thinking of the lesson the bird had taught him.

For none can live longer than the span allotted to him by Allah, whether he be only a bird or a great King.

The Ruby Ring

Once upon a time there was a King who went walking through the streets of his capital disguised as a Dervish to see the state of the city's affairs. Now, he had on an old, patched cloak and broken sandals, so that none knew him to be the ruler. But he had forgotten to take off a very fine ruby ring, the rarest in all the land and as he walked it shone in the sunshine like a drop of blood. A thief chanced to be coming behind the King and saw it. He thought to himself, 'Aha, that is a ring that I shall own before the night comes,' and he began to follow the King through the narrow markets, never letting him out of his sight. For he was a wicked man, who did not respect the belongings of others.

Now, in that city there were a great many fountains, with golden fish swimming about in large marble bowls. It was near the Grand Mosque, beside one of these tinkling fountains of clear cool water that the King stopped, when the heat of the afternoon was at its worst, to dip his hand in the marble bowl. As he did so his ring flew off and dropped into the water. The King did not notice. But the thief was watching and when the King moved away he plunged his hands into the water to see if he could get it out. But the ring was nowhere to be seen, which was not surprising, as a fish had swallowed it. Cursing his bad luck, the thief gave up the search and went off to rob a man whom he saw passing with an emerald hanging on a gold chain round his neck.

When the King got back to the Palace he realized

that he had lost his ring, but being a philosopher he said to himself, 'It is the Will of Allah that my ring has gone. Perhaps this is a way of showing me that I have too many possessions. Mysterious and wonderful are the ways of Allah.' And he went to bathe and change before visiting the Queen.

Now the Queen had a slave girl who was as brown as a nut, for she was from India, and her name was Leela. Leela was very fond of playing with the golden carp in the fountain in the courtyard of the Harem, and that day she took one of the fish out of the water, to stroke its golden scales. Just as she was about to drop it back in the fountain, the Queen's pet Persian cat jumped up and ate it. Then the cat ran away and lay at its mistress's feet, purring and washing its fur.

Leela was terrified, for there were always twelve fish in the Harem fountain, and each day her mistress counted them herself. What was to be done? The Queen had a very bad temper, and had warned Leela several times not to take the fish out of the water in case they should die. So, Leela veiled herself completely, picked up a small basin, and went to the Chief Eunuch. 'Let me pass, Agha, for I have to go and get some curd for my mistress,' she said, 'Here is the basin which I must bring it in, and quickly, or the Queen will have me beaten.' For none could leave or enter the Harem without permission of the Chief Eunuch.

'All right, girl, hurry on then, and be sure you are back by dark, or you will find the gate locked and barred,' cried the Eunuch.

Running as fast as her feet would carry her, Leela came to the fountain where the fish had swallowed the King's ring. Quick as a flash, she slipped one of the fish, with a little water to keep it alive, into the basin she carried.

When she got back to the Harem it was nearly

dark, and the Chief Eunuch was looking out for her.

'Hurry inside, my girl, I must lock the door,' he said crossly, peering at her with his large short-sighted eyes. Leela, holding her hand over the bowl to hide the fish from his gaze, tiptoed past him into the Harem, and the great door clanged shut. With a sigh of relief she dropped the fish into the alabaster fountain. There were now twelve fish swimming about in the shimmering water.

Strange as it may seem, this fish was the very same one which had swallowed the King's ring.

When he had bathed and changed into fresh clothes the King came to the Harem and enjoyed the company of his wife and three daughters, as they plied him with sweetmeats and sherbet.

'Oh, most Auspicious Lord,' said his lady, smiling, 'Where is the beautiful ruby ring, the finest in all Badakshan, which my father sent as a seal of our marriage pact twenty years ago?'

'Peace, wife,' answered the King, 'I lost it today, I do not know where, but it was while I wandered through the street, disguised as a wandering Dervish, to see the state of affairs. If Allah Wills that I should lose it, who am I to go against the Divine Will? Perhaps it is to teach me the futility of having too many worldly possessions.'

'Why, my Lord,' cried the Queen, 'amassing treasure for its own sake is unworthy, but that was a jewel which I would dearly love to see back on your finger. Let me summon my soothsayer and ask her to find out where the ring may have gone.'

The King tried to dissuade her, but the lady persisted, and in the end, when he saw there would be no peace until she had her way, he relented.

Then the King said to Leela, 'Go, bring the female Soothsayer here, and fetch her quickly, for I must get to the bottom of this matter tonight.'

So Leela hurried away to find the old woman, who

sat mumbling in her room, her tattered robe down to her ankles, and her white snakey locks covered with a crown of coins. When she could make the Soothsayer listen to her she said, 'Good mother, come quickly to the Harem. My mistress the Queen wants you to find the ruby ring my Lord and master lost today in the city.'

When the old Soothsayer came to the Harem she bowed low before the King and kissed the Queen's hands. She arranged her mystic charms on a tray, muttering to herself.

'What say you, Soothsayer,' asked the Lady, 'Where lies the ruby ring which my Lord lost today?'

And the Soothsayer answered, 'I can see—I can see—it is somewhere—somewhere dark.' She peered at her charms, then closed her eyes.

'Somewhere dark?' the Queen repeated, while the King looked on in amusement. 'Whatever do you mean?'

'Yes, yes, somewhere dark, and it is not far from this very spot. It is—it is at this moment in the Harem!'

'In the Harem? Why, you must be out of your wits, woman!' cried the Queen. 'It was in the streets of the city that the King lost the ring.'

'Yes, most gracious Lady, but it is now in the Harem, and was brought here soon after it was lost.'

'Somewhere dark,' mused the King, 'Is it in a cupboard?'

'No, my Lord, it is not.'

'Then is it in a bag?'

'No, my Lord, it is not.'

'Is it under the floor?'

'No, most Auspicious One, it is not, but it is surrounded by water... Ah, I have it,' the Soothsayer gave a cackle of triumph, 'It is in a fish!'

'In a fish? By my Faith!' shouted the King. 'This is the biggest jest I have ever heard!'

'Explain more fully,' commanded the Queen, 'How did it get into a fish in the first place?'

'My Lord's ring fell from his hand into a fountain near the Grand Mosque,' the Soothsayer intoned. 'A fish swallowed it, and the slave-girl Leela brought the fish here to replace the one the cat ate.' At this the old woman finished, and closed her eyes as if in sleep.

'Come here at once, Leela!' shrieked the Queen, 'How did the cat eat one of my fish? Were you playing with them again? What have you been doing? Explain this instant!'

So Leela threw herself at the King's feet and begged for his protection from the wrath of his lady. Then she kissed the hem of the Queen's robe and told what had happened, from beginning to end. 'And it was the fish with the blue fins which I picked out of the marble basin outside the Grand Mosque,' she sobbed. 'I can show you it, if you will have mercy upon me, great ones!'

The King smiled and looked at the angry Queen. 'I think we can allow this to pass for just one occasion,' said he. Then to the girl, 'Bring the fish and let us see if the ring is indeed inside.'

No sooner said than done, and as Leela held the golden carp in her hand, it coughed up the ring on to the floor. With a cry of joy the Queen picked up the gleaming ruby and put it back on the King's finger.

'Since Leela has been the means of bringing the fish here I will allow her action to go unpunished,' she said.

And the King caused the Soothsayer's mouth to be filled with gold, so that she went her way rejoicing.

Leela never touched the fish again, all the rest of her days.

The Beggar, the Lion and the Dog

There was once upon a time a poor man called Ahmad, who lived by begging. One day he met a girl who also was begging in the street, and she looked so ill and thin that he took pity upon her, saying, 'Oh, sister, come with me to my house and I will send for a doctor for you, so that you may, with Allah's help, very soon become better and not have to beg again. I will look after you like a brother.'

She said, 'Very well, I will come with you, but only if you marry me, for although I am an orphan, I am a virtuous girl. My name is Fatima. I do not want a brother, I need a husband.'

He agreed, and they went to the Kadi, who married them according to the law. Then very happily Ahmad took her to his home, a small shack in the poorest part of the city, and sent for the doctor.

The doctor said, 'This girl needs food and rest, she is exhausted and starving, so all I can prescribe is that you give her regular meals.'

Ahmad gave thanks to Allah and went out begging more than ever before to keep himself and his new wife, who daily grew more beautiful as she sat at home and ate heartily.

One day, when Ahmad was coming back from the Mosque where he had begged a good deal of money (it being a Friday and the weekly day of rest) he met a countryman in the street.

'Brother,' said the countryman, 'Give me a small sum of money and you shall have this bundle.'

'What is in it?' said Ahmad suspiciously, but he was very tempted.

'Buy it and see,' said the countryman, 'You will not regret it, I swear upon my beard!'

So Ahmad gave the man half of his coins and went on his way rejoicing, for he had a present to give his wife. She said, 'What is that you have with you?' and Ahmad replied, 'I do not know, I have just bought it from a countryman.'

Fatima opened the bundle. Inside she found a small brown dog. 'We shall keep it as a pet!' cried the bride.

'Oh, another mouth to feed,' grumbled Ahmad.

Crossly he went out to the public baths. When he had cleaned himself and put on a new pair of blue trousers and a red shirt, he strolled about in the street.

'O, Ahmad the Beggar!' called the barber from his booth. 'You should not be wearing red today. Have you not heard the Royal Proclamation?'

'No,' said Ahmad, 'I have been an hour or two in the baths since I got back from my day's work. What is the Proclamation?'

'His Majesty the King has decreed that no one shall wear red. He has a lion on a chain being taken through the streets this evening, and red will annoy the animal.'

'Rubbish!' said Ahmad. 'I don't care about that,' and he continued upon his walk.

Now forty soldiers were coming along holding a chain, on the end of which was the royal lion. When he saw Ahmad, the lion grew very angry and roared a mighty roar. The forty men were thrown to the ground and let go of the chain. The lion rushed at Ahmad, and struck at him with its paw. Ahmad seized a sword from one of the fallen soldiers and chopped the lion's head right off. Then the forty soldiers ran off to tell the King what had happened. All the people who had been watching from their windows called down, 'Allah have Mercy upon you,

O Beggar, for the King will have your life.'

But Ahmad said, 'Rubbish, I was only defending myself,' and he went on with his walk.

Then the forty soldiers of the King looked through all the streets of the town and found him and took him to the prison.

'The King has decreed that you shall stay here until he has forgiven you for cutting off the head of his lion', they said. 'You will be detained maybe for the rest of your life.'

So poor Ahmad, wondering what would happen to Fatima in his absence, was locked up in the prison until it should be the Monarch's pleasure to release him.

Now Fatima, watching and waiting for Ahmad, heard at last the news that he was in prison for cutting off the royal lion's head, and decided to go begging again to earn her living until he should return. So she put on her oldest, most tattered clothes and went to the steps of the Mosque.

'Alms in the name of Allah!' she cried shrilly, loudly and often, and soon she had several coins tied in a corner of her shawl. Every day from early until late she begged from the good people of the town and because she was so beautiful everyone gave her something. Every day the brown dog followed her and protected her from any harm. And after thirty days had passed the coins which Fatima had collected became a large sum of money, and she put this in a hole in the floor.

'Mistress Fatima,' said the dog to her one day, 'be not surprised that I can speak to you, for I am no ordinary cur. I was given this form by Suliman-Son-of-David, (upon Whom be Peace) whose creature I am. I was put in the world to be a dog until I should do a good deed for a human.'

'Are you a Jinn, then?' Fatima asked in surprise.

'Yes I am, and I want to give you some advice,

mistress. Go to the King and offer him the price of my master's freedom. You have enough money now, and the King's anger must have cooled. I am grateful to your husband, mistress, for did he not buy me from the countryman and save me from a worse fate? I might have been sold to a cruel man.'

'Yes,' Fatima answered, 'I will go to the King and ask for Ahmad to be pardoned.'

Putting all the money she possessed into a leather bag, she set off for the Palace, and the brown dog followed her. No sooner had she been admitted to the Hall of Audience in the Palace than the Grand Vizir took the money, saying, 'Go now, but come back again tomorrow; I will attend personally to your husband's case.'

So she went home. Next day when she returned to the Palace the servants said, 'The King has gone on a hunting expedition. There is no one here but the Grand Vizir.'

'Let me see him, then,' cried Fatima, 'for I want to ask him about my husband's release. He promised me yesterday, that he would look into the matter personally.'

The guards laughed. 'The Grand Vizir gave us orders that he was not to be disturbed today. He is entertaining people of high rank from foreign countries. Get away from here, beggar-girl, or you too will be put in prison.'

'Come, mistress Fatima,' whispered the brown dog. 'I have a plan.'

'But what can I do? The Grand Vizir has all my money,' wept Fatima. 'I shall never be able to help poor Ahmad now.'

'Listen to what I have to say,' said the dog. 'With the power invested in me by Suliman-Son-of-David, (upon Whom be Peace) whose creature I am, I can cause you to be borne into the Palace in a curtained litter, carried by four eunuchs.'

He barked three times, and Fatima found herself within a silken litter, slung from poles carried by four gigantic black eunuchs. She was dressed in beautiful silks and jewels. At her feet was the brown dog with a silver chain round its neck. The slaves carried Fatima right into the presence of the Grand Vizir, who was entertaining his foreign guests.

'Fatima, Princess of Turkestan,' cried the Eunuchs in unison. 'To pay homage to his Majesty the King.'

'Lady, I regret his Noble Majesty is away on a hunting expedition,' said the Vizir, looking admiringly at Fatima in her fine silken clothes and jewelled ornaments. 'But if you will give your slaves the order to bear you to the Royal Harem, everything will be prepared for your visit. You shall be entertained as a person of your style and rank until his Majesty returns.'

'What marvellous magic is this? What am I to do next?' Fatima whispered to the dog.

'Just behave as if you were indeed the Princess of Turkestan,' the enchanted creature answered.

So Fatima entered the Royal Harem and was greeted by the Queen and the seven daughters of the King and treated as an honoured guest.

Time passed, and the King returned from hunting, and when he came to the Harem to speak to his family he asked, 'Who is this most beautiful lady, and how did she arrive here?'

'Your Majesty,' said the Queen, 'This is Fatima, Princess of Turkestan, who is here on a visit.'

So the King gave instructions that a feast be prepared immediately in her honour.

'Do not smile, even if you want to,' said the brown dog, when the feast was in progress. Dancers and drummers, tambourine- and flute-players, tumblers and dwarfs all were brought to entertain the guest. But obeying the dog's instructions, Fatima did not smile, all through the proceedings. Even when she was given a morsel from the King's own plate as a sign of his favour, she sighed deeply.

'What is the matter, Princess of Turkestan?' said the King, 'Are you in some trouble?'

'Yes, most Imperial Majesty,' said Fatima. 'I am indeed, and that is why I have come to see you.'

'Ask me anything and it shall be immediately granted,' said the King. 'Begin at the beginning and tell me all, omitting no detail. Greatness does not isolate me from the needs of others.'

'Know, O Noble Majesty,' said Fatima, 'that my husband is in prison, and I gave all the money I possessed to an official, to beg for a free pardon for him.'

'Why, how monstrous!' exclaimed the King. 'This could never happen in my country.'

'It *has* happened here, O King,' said Fatima throwing herself at his feet. 'The official to whom I gave all my money was none other than your Grand Vizir, and the only way I could get to your royal presence was to come in disguise like this. For know, O King, that I am only a beggar-girl and my husband is Ahmad the Beggar who is in prison for having killed your Majesty's lion.'

'What! Is this true, Grand Vizir?' shouted the King in a rage, and as he looked at the Grand Vizir's face and trembling figure he knew it was indeed. Then, 'Seize him!' cried the King, 'and cast him out from the borders of this country, for I must have justice and honour in my Court.'

The Vizir grovelled on the floor. 'Forgive me, your Majesty, here is the bag of coins, I never meant to keep them, I only...'

'Silence, wretch!' bellowed the King. 'Go before I have you dragged away tied to the tails of wild asses. You are banished from my realm.'

Then the King raised up the tearful Fatima and told her that Ahmad would be given a pardon from that moment. Then he filled Fatima's bag with gold coins, so that neither she nor Ahmad had to beg again for the rest of their lives. Instead, they kept a small tea-house where travellers would come and refresh themselves, and were happy all their days. And Allah sent them many sons.

As for the Jinn in the shape of a brown dog, he returned to the Dominions of Suliman-Son-of-David, (upon Whom be Peace) for his good deed had earned him this remission of his sins.

The Water-Carrier's Fabulous Sons

There lived in a far-away part of Nuristan a poor water-carrier and his wife. Every day they lamented the fact that they had no children, and when his day's work was finished the water-carrier would go and sit under a walnut-tree and dream that he had three strong sons who would keep him in his old age.

One evening he said, 'O, Walnut-tree, if my wife and I had three sons to provide for our declining years, we would be the happiest people in the whole world.'

Now, he was sitting under a magical tree, and when he had finished speaking three walnuts fell to the ground beside him. They broke open, and in each was a perfectly-formed little boy, and each one called as he emerged, 'Here I am, Father, name me.'

So the water-carrier named them Mubarak, Mahsud and Rashid. He took them home to his wife, full of joy.

The miraculous boys grew up very fast, and soon they were taller and stronger than their human parents. The water-carrier said, 'Sons, you should go out into the world now and earn enough money to keep your mother and me in comfort for the rest of our days. Soon I shall be too old to carry water.'

So they set out, taking with them a goatskin of water and enough bread to last them a week. They walked on and on, until at the end of seven days they came to a great city. All the people were in mourning, and all the women in the street were crying.

'What is the matter in this city? Why is everyone

so sad?' asked Mubarak.

'Our King's three daughters have been stolen and we are all mourning for them, for the King is good and noble and the Princesses were the loveliest maidens in all the land,' said an old woman, snuffling into her veil.

Mubarak, Mahsud and Rashid went to the Palace and asked to see the Grand Vizir. 'Tell his Excellency we will find the Princesses,' said they.

'How dare you three poor lads come here and ask to see our Grand Vizir?' shouted the Captain of the Guard. 'Be off with you, or we shall cut your heads from your shoulders with swords of finest Damascus steel!'

At that moment the King came on his way to the Mosque, as it was Friday, and heard the three young men speaking. He held up his hand and asked them to address their questions to him.

'Your Majesty,' said Mubarak, 'My brothers and I would like to help to get the three Princesses back, for we have heard that they have been stolen. Tell us all about it, and we shall go and rescue them.'

The King was very astonished that three simple lads like these could come and speak so openly to him, and he liked them at once.

'My soldiers have looked everywhere, and my people are all in mourning, as you can see, so that if you can find my daughters anything you ask shall be yours,' he said. 'Blessings be upon you; may you find them soon.'

The three brothers were taken to the royal kitchens, and given enough provisions for a week. Then they set out to look for the three Princesses.

When they came to a cross-roads they sat down and began to discuss their plan of campaign.

'Let us make our camp here,' said Mahsud, 'and the first day one of us shall go out and look Westwards, and one of us Eastwards. The third will stay and cook the food and rest. The second day the others will go South and North, while the third stays to keep camp.' This they agreed, and it was so for a week. But there was no sign of the King's daughters, and nobody had any news in the four corners of the land which would help the brothers to find them.

When they all sat round the fire to have the last meal of the provisions they had brought with them, they saw coming into the firelight a little old man.

'Good evening, father,' said they together, 'Come and join us and warm yourself.'

'What are you cooking?' said the little old man, peering into the pot.

'This is a stew made from the last of our provisions,' said Mahsud, 'and now we shall have to go back to the King and tell him we have failed to find his daughters.'

'Give me a plateful of your food and I will tell you what to do,' said the little old man. So they piled his plate three times, until he had eaten nearly all there was, because they did not like to be impolite to a guest.

When he had eaten his fill, and was wiping his fingers on his beard, the little old man said, 'My sons, I know where the King's daughters are hidden; if you come with me I will show you.' He bade Mahsud take a burning stick from the fire to light their way.

So they left all their belongings and followed him into the darkness, and into a cave not far away. No sooner had they got into the cave than they heard a mocking laugh and the voice of the old man said, 'Hah-hah-hah, now I have you all in there, three young men and three Princesses, and I shall fatten you all up until I am ready to eat you.'

A door had closed over the opening. The three brothers looked around them, and in the light of the flare which Mahsud was holding they saw the trembling figures of three beautiful girls huddled in the corner of the cave.

'Have no fear, Princesses, we have come to save you,' whispered Mahsud. 'My brothers and I have been sent by your father the King to look for you.'

'But we are all prisoners,' cried the eldest Princess. 'Our hands and feet are tied and we are faint from being held captive in this dreadful cave.'

No sooner had she finished speaking than there was another mocking laugh from outside of the cave and their captor said, 'No need to tell these silly young men all about it, my dear, they are as captive as you.' And then there was the sound of the little old man scampering away.

Mahsud said again, 'Listen, Princesses, my brothers and I are no ordinary men, for we were born of a magic walnut-tree, and we are possessed of the power to escape from any place where we may be held, by virtue of our extraordinary strength. Look!' And as the girls watched in amazement, the three brothers pushed at the great cave-door with all their might, and it opened.

Then Mubarak untied the three Princesses' hands and feet, so that they were able to come out of the cave and go back to the camp where the three brothers had prepared their meal. There was just enough left in the pot from them all to have a little soup, and as it was a bright moonlit night, they decided to return to the Palace before the little old man discovered they had escaped.

By dawn next day the three brothers and the three Princesses were within sight of an oasis, when they looked back and saw a very small cloud in the distance.

'Brothers, cover the Princesses with our cloaks, for I do not like the look of that dust,' said Mubarak. But almost as he had finished speaking the little old man had appeared in their midst, riding a racing camel which was as fast as the wind.

'Stop!' cried the little old man. 'You are my prisoners, and I shall cast a spell upon you. Turn into pure gold, all of you.'

Now, the Princesses, being mortal, were turned into golden statues, and fell forward on to the ground, but the three brothers who had been born of the magical walnut-tree each said a magic word and kept their own shape. The little old man screamed with rage, and lashed out at them in anger, but the three brothers shouted together, 'In the name of Suliman-Son-of-David (upon Whom be Peace) disappear!' and the little old man and the camel vanished into thin air. So they took up the Princesses who had turned into pure gold and sprinkled over them a little water from a goatskin pouch, and the girls became human again.

The sun was getting hotter and hotter, and their feet sank into the sand, until they could walk no further. So when they reached an oasis Mubarak said, 'We had better rest here, for we cannot combat the heat of the sun, even with the power invested in us by Suliman-Son-of-David, (on Whom be Peace) whose slaves we are.' And the Princesses lay down gratefully on the ground, and drank, and bathed their feet, until the sun grew less hot.

Now, a band of bandits came riding to that oasis to water their camels, and they saw the six travellers and were very curious about them. 'Where are you from, strangers, and whither are you bound?' they asked suspiciously.

'We are from such-and-such a place, brother, and are going to such-and-such a place,' said Mahsud, Mubarak and Rashid.

The bandits were most annoyed that they had not been told every detail of the business, and decided to attack them as soon as night fell. But just as they were about to do so the three brothers said with one voice, 'Fly away, O Evil ones, right into the sky!' and a great wind arose up and blew the bandits and their camels right out of sight, up into the starry sky. And for all I know, they are whirling about up there to this very day.

As soon as dawn came the three brothers roused the Princesses from their sleep and said a magic word. A camel with six humps came up out of nowhere. The camel sat down and each of them jumped up and sat on a hump, and the huge camel rose to its feet and galloped off with them to the Palace. No sooner had they arrived at the gate than the Captain of the Guard and his soldiers ran out, and helped the three Princesses to the ground. No sooner had the three brothers jumped to earth than the six-humped camel vanished, and all the astonished townspeople who were watching rubbed their eyes with astonishment.

Weary and dusty, the Princesses were taken to the harem to be bathed, dressed and scented, and the three brothers were given every honour by the King as soon as he heard the news of his daughters' return.

That night there was a feast the like of which the city had never seen before, and Mubarak, Mahsud and Rashid sat in places of honour near the King himself.

'Young men,' said the King, 'In the midst of all this assembly I ask you to name anything you like, and it shall be yours for bringing back my dear daughters when nobody in the land could find them.'

'Noble King,' said Mahsud, 'I want nothing.'

'Noble King,' said Mubarak, 'I want nothing.'

'Noble King,' said Rashid, 'I want nothing.'

'Well said!' cried the King. 'Cause their mouths to be filled with gold and jewels!' And all the courtiers cheered when the royal treasurer was summoned, and the three brothers had their mouths filled with gold and gems of great price.

Now, the three Princesses wanted to marry the three young men who had saved them, and the King agreed, but Mubarak, Mahsud and Rashid wanted to get back to the old water-carrier and his wife who had brought them up, to give them the gold and jewels.

'This will keep them in plenty for the rest of their days,' they said, for they were very fond of the old couple. So while the three Princesses were getting ready to have a triple wedding, the three young men left in a hurry, sending them each a golden walnut with this message inside:

> 'A Princess cannot marry me
> For I was born of a walnut-tree.'

No sooner had Mubarak, Mahsud and Rashid given the old water-carrier and his wife the full story of their adventures and presented them with the treasure, than the three bade their foster-parents good-bye, because they felt the urge to travel once more. And for all I know, they are travelling yet, for the old water-carrier and his wife never saw them again.

The Faithful Gazelle

Once upon a time there was a poor beggar who slept upon the outside oven of a rich man's kitchen. One morning he was awakened by the cries of a vendor who was calling, 'Gazelles! Gazelles! Buy my fine gazelles!'

The beggar said, 'There is no one awake at this hour in the rich man's house. Cease your noise until a more civilised hour, brother.'

The gazelle-seller, who had several of the poor creatures in a cage on top of a donkey cart, replied:

'Would you like to buy one of these fine gazelles?'

'I have only a handful of coppers,' said the beggar, 'What would I do with a gazelle, anyway?' And he climbed down off the oven to talk to the gazelle-seller.

At that moment one of the small animals poked its head out of the cage and said in a low voice to the beggar, whose name was Mustapha, 'Buy me, and you will not be sorry.'

Mustapha was so astonished that he said to the gazelle-seller, 'Here is all I have in the world—three copper coins. Can I buy this gazelle with its head out of the cage for that?'

'Take it and be blessed!' cried the man, and released the gazelle. 'As I shall only have to feed the thing, I shall let it go for whatever you can give me.' Then he closed the cage again, took three coppers from Mustapha, and went on his way to the nearest tea-house.

'Well,' said Mustapha to the gazelle, 'what about

it? I have bought you, and now I have nothing left in the world, until I can get something more, sitting on the steps of the mosque at the time of the midday prayer.'

'You will not regret buying me,' said the gazelle, 'for I shall make your fortune.'

'How is that?' cried Mustapha, 'and what shall I do next?'

'Do nothing, simply stay here until I return,' said the gazelle, and it trotted away.

The tattered beggar scratched his head. He would probably never see the wretched animal again, he thought. How did he allow himself to be so deluded as to give three copper coins for a talking gazelle? Probably the creature was bewitched, and might bring him bad luck. So ruminating, he sat down again on the oven to wait until the rich man's servants woke, and then perhaps they would throw out some food that he could eat.

Meanwhile, the gazelle ran on until it reached the house of a noble prince. It bowed to him and said, 'O Prince of a Thousand Blessings, I am the slave of a great and noble merchant, whose caravan has just been attacked and plundered by thieves. Could you please send some clothes for him to put on, so that he may not have to appear before you completely naked when he comes to pay you a visit?'

'Certainly, good gazelle,' said the Prince, 'My servant shall give you a white linen shirt and a robe of the finest wool to take to your master. And when he has recovered from his shock, let him come here to my house, so that I may cause a sheep to be roasted in his honour.'

The gazelle thanked the Prince and said, 'I was to bring you this emerald in payment of any clothes which you might send, as my master does not wish to accept your kindness for nothing.' Thereupon the gazelle placed a perfect emerald without flaw at the feet of the prince, and bounded away with the clothes upon its back.

The Prince was delighted at the value of the gift, and resolved that if the man did appear he would offer him the hand of his daughter, for he was apparently a person of some substance.

The gazelle went back to Mustapha and said, 'Look, I have brought you these clothes from a wealthy prince. Cast off your rags, bathe in the river, and put on these magnificent garments.'

The beggar was amazed and said, 'How in the world did you manage to do this? Never in my life have I seen such beautiful clothes.'

'Do as I tell you,' said the gazelle, 'and I shall get you a rich wife as well. Did you not give me back my liberty by buying me from the man who had put me in a cage?'

The long and the short of it was that the clothes transformed the beggar into a man who could sit in any Royal Court without shame.

'Now, follow me,' said the gazelle, and trotted off into a ruined building. 'Look under the third brick on the left and you will see a treasure.'

Sure enough, as Mustapha lifted the brick he saw the gleam of gold and precious stones in a cavity below. So he filled his pockets and his money-belt, until he had as much as he could carry.

'What a piece of luck!' cried the beggar. 'I shall never have to go without anything for the rest of my days.'

'Not if you marry into the family of the prince,' said the gazelle. 'Buy yourself a horse, and riding boots, and we shall set out for the noble prince's house at once.'

An hour later Mustapha, mounted on a beautiful white horse, followed the gazelle as it sped along like the wind before him. Soon they reached a tall house with many carved balconies, surrounded by a beautiful garden.

'Wait here,' said the gazelle, 'until I come for you; and remember that you are now a rich merchant whose caravan has been set upon by thieves and plundered.'

'I understand,' said Mustapha. 'I shall stay here until you return.'

The gazelle then went to the inner courtyard of the house, and presenting itself to the Prince let fall a priceless ruby without flaw at his feet, saying, 'My master, the noble Mustapha, sends you blessings and peace, and requests that he may call upon you at once, to thank you for the clothes you sent him after his recent misfortune. In the meantime, here is a small token of his regard which he wishes to give to you as a mark of his respect.'

'Excellent gazelle!' cried the Prince. 'Let your master hasten here as fast as he can, for I am eager to meet him, and he should start thinking of himself as my future son-in-law from this moment.'

The gazelle returned to Mustapha and acquainted him with what the Prince had said, and soon the one-time beggar and the rich and venerable Prince were sitting together drinking tea like old friends. By nightfall, when the sheep had been roasted and eaten, the Prince came to the delicate subject of his daughter. 'My son,' said he, placing his hand on Mustapha's arm, 'I am glad that I have kept my daughter until you came, for I can think of no more suitable match for her. I shall arrange for the marriage rites to be solemnised tomorrow, and she shall come to you with her servants and her dowry all complete.'

At this news the one-time beggar was delighted, and thanked his lucky stars for bringing him to such good fortune.

Next day, at the wedding, he was congratulated by every member of the family, who each piled gifts before the happy pair. The bridal feast went on for hours, and at last they were led to a bedroom hung with rare carpets and decorated with lamps of burnished brass set with coral. While they slept the gazelle lay across the threshold, keeping watch.

The months passed. The Prince had to go on a journey, so he gave his daughter and new son-in-law the grand house to live in until his return. There were tinkling fountains in blue-tiled courtyards, carved wooden balconies, vast rooms with painted pillars. Mustapha became more and more conceited, and forgot completely what he owed to the gazelle. He spent all day playing knuckle-bones with his new friends.

One day the gazelle went to its mistress and said, 'Lady, ask my master if he will give me a bowl of curds and honey, prepared with his own hands, for I am feeling ill, and fear that I may die.'

So the girl went to her husband and said, 'Peace and blessings be upon you, husband. Please give the gazelle a bowl of curds and honey prepared with your own hands as it is ill and fears that it may die.'

And the man answered, 'Foolish one, do not worry about the animal. Did I not buy it for only a few pence? Take no notice, and leave me to my game of knuckle-bones.'

Then the girl went back to the gazelle, which was lying on the ground looking very weak and thin, and said, 'I cannot get your master to come. Shall I prepare you the mixture myself, so that you will get better?'

The gazelle said, 'No, mistress, thank you. I would rather that my master did it. Please go back to him and beg him for my sake to do as I ask, or I shall die.'

So she ran back to Mustapha and said, 'Come quickly, the gazelle begs you to do as it asks, or indeed it will die, for it is now so weak and thin, lying on the ground.'

But again her husband would not do anything, and told her to go to the gazelle and give it a bowl of milk herself.

When the girl got back to where the gazelle was lying she saw its eyes were dull, and when she had told it Mustapha was not coming, it dropped its head and died.

That night, lying in his luxurious bedroom, the man who had been a beggar said to his wife, 'What happened to the gazelle? You did not come back to tell me.'

She answered sadly, 'It died, and I am so grieved at the way you disregarded the poor creature's pleas that I have decided when my father comes back I shall take my dowry and return to my family, for I no longer love you. What a disappointment you have been to me.'

'Foolish woman!' cried Mustapha. 'Go to sleep, and in the morning you will have forgotten all about this matter.' Within a few moments he was snoring.

In the middle of the night he had a dream. He thought he saw the gazelle again, and its eyes were very sad. 'Why did you not bring me a bowl of curds and honey when I begged you to do so? Had you forgotten that you owed all your good fortune to me? I was grateful because you bought my liberty back for me, why could you not show me one act of kindness when I was in need?'

'I asked my wife to take you a bowl of milk!' cried Mustapha, feeling suddenly very ashamed of himself.

'It was not the same thing,' said the gazelle, faintly, and it disappeared.

In a great fright, Mustapha sat up, and found himself Mustapha the beggar again, dressed in tatters, sitting against the oven of a rich man's house in the moonlight. And he remained a beggar for the rest of his life.

The Leopard and the Jinn

Once upon a time there was a King and he was feasting one night with all his courtiers. Now at the feast was a foreign Emissary, who asked permission of the King to return to his own country the following day.

'By all means, go, and peace be with you, but do not forget,' said the King graciously, 'to take our present to your Sultan, which goes to him with our most brotherly affection.'

'What present, Most Auspicious One?' said the Emissary, half afraid of what it could be, for the King was one inclined to practical jokes in rather dubious taste, and he feared that it might have been a giantess, or perhaps a cannibal of very short stature.

'Why, my most beautiful and well-trained leopard, of course,' laughed the King and clapped his hands for his Head Huntsman.

In came the Huntsman, with a very elegant leopard on a golden chain which he presented to the Emissary on the King's instructions.

'May you live for ever, O King,' said the Emissary, faintly.

'A thousand thanks, on behalf of my royal master.'

Taking the chain, he led the leopard away to his own chamber. The animal seemed docile enough, and did not appear to be at all unwilling to be led about by someone who was not its usual keeper.

The Emissary, whose name was Jalaludin, prayed to Allah that he could keep the leopard in good humour for the journey.

All next day they travelled, and all the day after, until they were not far from a wayside inn, where people were lodged for the night. Jalaludin was leading the leopard, and feeling very footsore and weary, when he saw coming along the road the keeper of the inn, taking his daily stroll.

'Good day, brother,' said Jalaludin, 'I am looking forward to resting at the inn at last after my three days' journey with only this leopard for company. Have you a bed ready that I may be able to settle down and get a good sleep before we have to go on our way again tomorrow?'

'Good friend,' said the inn-keeper, 'go ahead and rest in the inn by all means, but, I beg you, do not take that leopard in, for it will frighten everyone already staying there, and might kill the goats and chickens they are keeping for provisions. If you want to have a bed there tonight, you will have to dispose of the leopard at once.'

'But this magnificent animal is a present from the King to my master the Sultan,' cried Jalaludin. 'I cannot dispose of it as you say. If the King sends my master a letter, asking how his leopard fares, and I have killed it before presenting it to His Excellency, why, he would personally strike my head from my shoulders without even asking me what had happened.'

'I see' nodded the inn-keeper, 'but I cannot allow the animal near my lodgers. However, to save you sleeping out in the open, and having to put up with the dangers of wolves or thieves tonight, you may sleep at a small house which I own just outside the town. This house, unfortunately, is inhabited by an evil Jinn, which gives those who live in the house no peace. It is forever rattling chains, and moaning or screeching, breaks china and moves furniture about, until it has become impossible to live there. Now if you go there, you must take no notice of the Jinn, and I dare say it will take no notice of the leopard.'

Jalaludin thanked the man, and was directed to the house.

'Perhaps the Jinn will not be at home tonight,' thought he, leading the leopard up to the door and lifting the latch. Inside the house, which was clean and swept, there were a few plates and dishes lying broken on the table. However, Jalaludin was so tired he lay down at once on the bed, and let the leopard leap up on to the quilt beside him. He fastened its chain to one of the posts of the bed, and soon both were fast asleep.

Just as the moon rose and the owls began to hoot, the door of the house opened and the Jinn appeared. Howling with laughter, and making the floors shake with its huge feet, the Jinn began to eat a goat which it had skinned, and all this activity caused the Emissary to wake up. He looked in horror as the Jinn, which was venomously ugly, with a face like a demon, and, with teeth which protruded like fangs, chewed pieces of the goat, and tore at the flesh with long talons. Jalaludin could scarce believe his eyes when he saw the dreadful creature.

Suddenly the leopard woke, and leapt from the bed, its golden chain rattling and its eyes blazing with rage.

'Ha-ha-ha!' said the Jinn, 'What is this stupid spotted cat doing here?'

The leopard, which had been so quiet and well-mannered all the time it had been travelling with the Emissary, now began to snarl, showing its teeth in a most dangerous way. Then a fierce battle began. This way and that flew tables and stools, pots and pans, and Jalaludin watched with horror as the Jinn and the leopard bit and clawed each other, with the most fearsome roars, growls and grunts. One minute the Jinn would be on top, then the leopard, and soon it was obvious that the Jinn was getting the worst of it. Peeping out of the cupboard where he had hidden at the height of the fray, Jalaludin saw the leopard with one last fierce swipe of its paw strike such a blow that the Jinn went howling up the chimney, out of sight.

'My brave leopard, you are indeed a good fighter,' cried Jalaludin, leading the now purring animal back to bed, where both lay down and slept the rest of the night in peace.

Next morning the inn-keeper was early at the door with some bread and milk, wondering how things had fared in the night.

'Brother, thank you for the shelter of this pleasant house, the blessings of Allah be upon you,' said Jalaludin as he shared the milk with the leopard, who was contentedly washing face and paws in the sunlight.

'B-but what about the Jinn?' cried the astonished inn-keeper, 'Was there no sign of the evil creature last night?'

'Certainly, brother,' responded the Emissary airily, 'but this excellent leopard soon got rid of that demon. There was a wonderful fight and the Jinn escaped up the chimney. I doubt if you will be worried by it again.'

'A thousand thanks!' said the other. 'Take the rest of these provisions for the next stage of your journey, and may Allah lengthen your days.'

With the man's heartfelt blessings ringing in his ears, Jalaludin took the leopard's golden chain and set off along the road.

That night they reached some caves, and sheltered there when darkness fell, huddling together for warmth. No sooner had midnight come, than Jalaludin awoke and saw the evil figure of the Jinn in the entrance of the cave.

'Human being!' bellowed the Jinn, 'I have tracked

you down by the power invested in me by Suliman, Son of David, (upon Whom be Peace). Come outside and let me devour you, for you must be punished because your great spotted cat drove me out of a very comfortable house which I much enjoyed.'

No sooner had he finished, than the leopard woke up with a start, and Jalaludin could not hold on to the chain. So he let it go, and saw the leopard leap upon the Jinn as if it were nothing but a piece of old leather, shaking it as a dog shakes a rat. Howling with pain, the Jinn ran away, and the sinuous leopard, purring with pleasure, came back to lie against Jalaludin's side in the cave.

'Oh, my brave animal, however shall I thank you?' said Jalaludin, and soon they were both asleep.

Next day they set off again, and at last arrived at the spice-scented land from which Jalaludin had set off so long ago. All the people cheered to see the Emissary with the beautiful docile leopard on its golden chain, as he walked to the Palace of the Sultan.

Jalaludin, returning home after so long in a foreign land, wept with joy to see his own countrymen again, and though he was sorry to part with the leopard, he took it to the Court to give to the Sultan.

When the nobles saw the animal they shrank back and one or two took to their heels, but the leopard merely padded along beside Jalaludin looking at them pleasantly with its golden eyes.

'O Great Sultan!' cried Jalaludin, prostrating himself before the throne. 'Here, from the King of a Thousand Suns, comes a rare leopard as a present to your Augustness.'

'What!' bellowed the Sultan, twirling his moustache, 'A leopard! A wild creature like that as a pet! Know, that while you have been gone, the King of the Ethiopians has sent me two lions, on excellent terms with each other, to be my bodyguards. If I were to introduce this fierce-looking leopard into the Court the fur might certainly begin to fly.'

At his words there entered the Lion Master with two fine young lions, each on a strong chain. The leopard's tail began to swish, and its eyes grew into large, glistening orbs. Jalaludin found he had to use all his strength to pull the animal back, for it was beginning to growl in rage at the sight of the lions.

'Jalaludin, take the leopard as a gift, with my thanks for your task well done,' said the Sultan hastily. 'But get that animal out of here. Take it, and with my blessings, for it would be one cat too many among those already at my court.'

Breathlessly, Jalaludin thanked the Sultan, then hurried the leopard away, and returned to his own house.

He bathed and changed and lay on his divan, and the servants brought him spiced rice with meat-balls to eat. At his feet, looking at him with love and devotion, sat the beautiful spotted leopard, now at peace with all the world.

'Dearest leopard,' said Jalaludin happily, as he dried his hands upon a napkin when the servant had cleared away the meal, 'Allah be praised that the Sultan has seen fit to give you to me, for after our adventures together I could wish for no better companion than you for the rest of my life.'

'O Excellent master!' cried the leopard in a musical voice, 'It rejoices my heart to hear your words, for they will set me free from my bondage. Know, O Worthy Jalaludin, that I am no ordinary leopard, but a princess who was bewitched by a wicked magician when I was but seventeen in my father's house in faraway Tashkand. Say that you are free and willing to marry me, and I shall turn into a woman again before your very eyes.'

'Bless my beard!' cried Jalaludin. 'Am I hearing right? Why, of course I am free and willing to marry you to release you from the spell, and we shall celebrate our wedding this very night.'

So, at his words, the leopard changed into a beautiful young woman, with long shiny black hair and almond-shaped eyes, and a yellow gown made of spotted silk, which came to her ankles. Around her waist was a belt studded with precious stones, and on her head a jewelled cap of golden mesh.

Jalaludin was smitten with love for her, and they were married in great joy. So Allah sent them many sons, and Jalaludin and the Princess of Tashkand lived happily together until the end of their days.

Prince Mahsud and King Rat

Once upon a time there was a King of Afghanistan who had twin children, a girl called Fatima and a boy named Mahsud. At the Palace they sat on each side of their father's throne when he was holding audience, and played together in the royal garden every day.

Now, one morning they were throwing a golden ball to each other among the rose-beds, when the ball fell into a clump of roses and was lost.

'Brother,' cried Fatima, 'There seems to be a huge hole in this part of the garden where there was not one yesterday. What can it mean?'

'Let us go down the hole,' said Mahsud, 'the ball must have fallen into it.' And he took his sister's hand as they stepped down into the darkness. For a few moments they stood blinking in the entrance of an underground cave, then suddenly it was illuminated with a thousand tiny lights.

'Come in, my dear ones,' said a kind voice, as they stared in surprise. 'If you are looking for your ball, here it is, for it has rolled into my dwelling-place.'

'Who are you?' said Mahsud, as Fatima clung to him in fear, 'Give us our ball back, and we shall leave you in peace.'

At that moment there was a flicker of light more bright than any of the others, and they saw a rat, sitting on a tiny throne. 'Welcome to my audience chamber,' said the rat, 'I am King Rat, who rules over all the rats of this region. My miners are, as you see, working with might and main to repair this hole beneath your garden.' Then the children saw that each light was carried by a rat, and that there were a hundred or more of these creatures tunnelling further into the ground.

The golden ball was lying right under the throne, and Mahsud stooped to pick it up. 'Thank you, King Rat,' said he politely, 'We have invaded your underground palace and we apologise, but as you see, we did not know...'

The rat raised one of its paws and stopped him. 'Pray think nothing of it, we should have this cleared up by tomorrow. But may I ask you one favour?'

'Certainly, please ask anything,' said Mahsud.

'Try to keep your gardeners from finding us until we have another tunnel dug, and then we shall fill in this hole to cover our dwelling-place completely.' So the children promised, and bade King Rat farewell.

When they were back in the sunlight again Mahsud said to his sister, 'Go to the head gardener, and tell him that he should take all his gardeners to cut roses for the harem from the other side of the Palace, and I will stay here to turn them away if they should chance to come in this direction.'

Fatima ran to the head gardener and said, 'Please take all your gardeners and collect roses for the harem from the other side of the Palace, for I would like my mother the Queen to have as many roses as you can carry to her, as a surprise from me.'

So the gardeners did as she bid them, for she was the King's only daughter, and young as she was, her slightest wish was always granted.

By the time the roses were cut and arranged in baskets and taken to the harem, it was nearly dark. Mahsud, who had been keeping watch near the hole saw it was rapidly becoming filled with earth. When it was finished, Mahsud went back to the Palace and joined his sister at the evening meal.

'Is everything all right, brother?' Fatima whispered to him as he sat beside her. He nodded, and reached out for his helping of spiced rice with mutton.

Next day, when they were playing in the garden again with the golden ball, a strange-looking ragged beggar-woman looked through a hole in the garden wall, where some bricks were missing, and said, 'Give me a coin to buy food, royal ones, I am starving, for I have not eaten for days. Have pity upon me!'

Then Fatima said to her brother, 'Give the poor woman the golden ball, Mahsud, for that is all we have got. She can sell it in the market and buy some food with it.' Mahsud agreed and held out the ball of gold to the tattered old woman. No sooner had the beggar-woman snatched the ball from the young prince, than she caught hold of his hand too, and pulled him, struggling, towards her, through the hole in the wall. He tried to pull his hand away, but she was a female Jinn, and very strong, so before Fatima's horrified eyes she thrust Mahsud into a sack and galloped away with him like the wind, laughing fiendishly. Fatima got through the hole in the wall as quickly as she could, but when she at last managed it there was no sign of the Jinn or her brother. She ran back to the Palace and told the King what had happened, between her sobs.

'Captain of the Guard!' roared the King, 'Get every man in the kingdom out, and look for my son. When you find the wretched beggar-woman who abducted him, beat the soles of her feet with split bamboos!'

But though the soldiers searched the length and breadth of the town and all the country round, no trace of the young prince could be found.

Fatima was sitting in the garden near the roses, weeping as if her heart would break, when suddenly she saw a rat pop up from a small hole at her feet.

'Greetings to you, Princess, from my lord, King Rat,' squeaked the rat, 'I have come to deliver a message of good tidings.'

'Nothing which does not concern the return of my twin brother can be good tidings to me,' cried Fatima, with red eyes.

'It *is* concerning your brother, the Prince,' cried the rat. 'My lord, King Rat, bids me inform you that he knows where the prince has been taken, and by whom, and that he is soon to be rescued by one of us, so take courage.' And with that, the rat disappeared back into its hole.

Drying her eyes, Fatima ran back to the Palace and told her parents, though they found it hard to believe her.

Now, as soon as the Jinn had stolen Mahsud, she took him to her lair, which was a deep, dry well on the outskirts of the kingdom. She hung the sack containing the young prince on a hook and, cackling with delight, began to examine the golden ball, which seemed to give her great joy. She threw herself down onto a thick pile of animal skins and was soon snoring, the golden ball in one huge hand.

No sooner was she sound asleep than Mahsud, who had been peeping through a rent in the sack, saw a rat come hopping along on its hind legs, from a hole right at the bottom of the wall.

'Listen, young Prince,' squeaked the rat. 'I have come to save you. My lord, King Rat, has sent me to gnaw a hole in the sack and help you to escape.' And it began to chew with its sharp teeth at the bottom of the sack. It gnawed and gnawed, and in about half an hour the hole was big enough for Mahsud to crawl through and jump down on to the ground.

Just as Mahsud was beginning to thank him, the rat said, 'Quickly, we have no time to talk, for I have been tunnelling beneath here for the last twelve hours, and the water should be returning soon to the well. We must climb out of here before the Jinn wakens.'

'My golden ball!' cried Mahsud, reaching out to take it from the ogress's hand.

'Hush,' whispered the rat, 'Do not touch it, for she will wake before we can escape. Have patience, your ball will float to the top when the well fills with water.'

So Mahsud and the rat climbed up the ladder on the inside of the well, and when they reached the very last rung the Jinn awakened with a scream of rage. At that moment, the waters rose from the bottom of the well, and the evil female Jinn was drowned. Then, as Mahsud watched, the golden ball floated to the surface.

'Your father's soldiers will be here soon,' said the rat, as it prepared to disappear into a small hole in the sand. 'In the meantime, blessings from my lord, King Rat, and if you are ever in any trouble, call one of us and we shall do whatever is in our power.' So saying, it vanished.

Mahsud, holding his golden ball in his hand, looked at the horizon, where there was a tiny dust-cloud no bigger than a man's hand. As he watched, the cloud grew bigger and bigger, and the army appeared, riding their fastest horses, looking for him. He waved his arms, and the Captain of the Guard called to the troops to stop, which they did with much joy, seeing that their prince was found.

So Mahsud rode back with the soldiers, laughing for sheer delight at being alive.

Then the King gave a great feast, which lasted for seven days, and seven nights, and offering thanks to Allah, slaughtered many sheep, which were divided among the poor.

The Amir who was a Beggar

Once upon a time there was a great and noble Amir who became so proud and haughty that he forgot how to rule his people wisely. Instead of ruling them with care and understanding, he grew more and more interested in the riches which poured into the state coffers from taxes and fines. His courtiers were so occupied in flattering the ruler that no one spoke the truth to him, or advised him about the true position. Therefore he thought only of money, jewels, and fine clothes, forgetting the simple things of life.

There were a thousand slaves in the royal palace, black and white, young and old, and daily they prayed to Allah to save them from the tyranny of the Amir. Now, one night, when the moon was full in the sky, and the stars shone with a frosty light, the Amir had a dream. It seemed to him that he was in a strange place, where there was inexpressible peace and serenity. An angel, writing in a book with a golden pen, appeared and said, 'O unfaithful Amir, Servant of Allah, why do you oppress your people and forget the teachings of the Koran?'

And the Amir answered, 'I cannot understand the meaning of these words. How can I be an oppressor?... I have the loyalty of a thousand slaves, black and white, old and young, and everyone in the kingdom bows to me when I pass by.'

The Vision spoke again. 'Change everything about yourself, or you will regret it. Thinking, doing, living, all must change.'

Then the Amir saw the angel write again in the

golden book, and vanish.

Next day, early, the Amir was determined to enjoy himself. He ordered all the finest horses in his stables to be saddled, so that he and the entire Court could go hawking. The nobles and huntsmen were dressed in magnificent robes of honour, and their hawks had jewelled hoods. The hunting cheetahs were brought as well, and soon they began to chase the game. One cheetah went off so fast after a gazelle that none but the Amir could follow it on his Arabian stallion. Further and further ran the gazelle, with the cheetah after it, and the Amir following behind, so that soon all the courtiers and huntsmen were left far in the distance. The Amir spurred on his horse, and suddenly the cheetah stopped, puzzled. The gazelle had vanished. The Amir dismounted, and looked about him. Where could the animal have gone? It seemed to have disappeared into thin air.

All at once a great wind blew up, and it blew and blew, until the Amir was nearly blinded. He hung on to the horse's bridle, but it seemed as if the wind was about to blow them off the face of the earth. His cloak and head-covering were whipped off, his body was stung as if by a thousand whips. He shaded his eyes with his hands to protect them, and the horse, neighing with fright, galloped away. The Amir was in a terrible state, his eyes were burning with the stinging sand, his clothes were tattered and torn, and his hair tangled like that of a dancing dervish. He was utterly lost, and alone, without money or servants.

'What am I to do?' he groaned, sinking to his feet, and his senses left him.

For a time he knew no more, until he opened his eyes to find that a Nomad was bending over him, giving him a drink from a water-skin.

'How did I get here? My head seems possessed by a thousand demons,' faltered the Amir trying to get up. He was lying on a pile of skins, in a Nomad encampment.

'Rest, brother, rest,' said the Nomad. 'You were found not far from this place by one of our children, after yesterday's sandstorm. You will be all right now, you can come with us when we move our flocks to follow the grazing.'

'But I am the Amir. I insist that you take me back to my Palace.' He tried to rise.

'What! You the Amir? In that torn and dirty shirt and one sandal? Surely you must be affected by the sun-madness. We are miles away from the Amir's city, and as for his Palace, none of us has ever seen it, for there is a high wall around it guarded by soldiers. It is as much as our lives are worth to go to the Palace, let alone take you with us and tell them that you are the Amir!' And the Nomad roared with laughter.

In two days' time the Amir recovered his strength, and he was given a brown sheepskin coat by his host. He could not believe what had happened to him, but hoped that in time he might be able to find his way back to his own kingdom. When the tribe of Nomads moved on, they took him with them, promising to show him where the nearest town lay. He trudged along, with hope in his heart, and arrived at last at the huge iron gate of his own Palace.

'Stop, you tattered rascal!' shouted the guard. 'This is the residence of our most noble and worthy ruler. Get back to the steps of the mosque, where you belong.'

'But I am the Amir. Let me in, for I have been lost in the wilderness since I went hunting, and after being rescued by a Nomad, I have now returned. Open the gate this instant or I shall have you whipped.'

'What an impudent beggar you are. I swear by my beard that you shall be whipped yourself if the

Captain of the Guard comes out to you!' roared the soldier, and pushed the wretched Amir away.

'I tell you, I am the Amir. Send for the Captain of the Guard, and I will identify myself,' shouted the unfortunate potentate.

'Our noble Amir is at this very moment on his knees in the Palace courtyard, for it is the time of the noonday prayer,' said the soldier. 'See for yourself, look through the gate at the right and watch the Lord of the Faithful place his forehead to the ground in obeisance to Allah.'

Sure enough, the Amir squinted through the gate and looked to the right as the soldier bade him, and there he saw a figure, dressed in *his* clothes, and wearing his ruby ring, kneeling upon a prayer-rug. He knew at once that this must be an angel, for around the figure there seemed to be a golden light.

Thunderstruck, he wandered from the Palace, and went through the streets, like a man in a trance. Since it was so long since he had been known to his people no one recognised their Amir and evidently they accepted the angel as their ruler without question.

So the Amir who was now a beggar, travelled from mosque to mosque, asking for alms, for he had never learned how to do anything but hunt or ride. Day by day he grew stronger, until he was able to carry bundles for women shopping in the market, or hold horses for merchants, earning a few coppers a day. At nights he slept against the outside ovens of the houses of the rich, and soon gave up all hope of ever being known as the Amir again.

Each Friday the new Amir distributed food and money to the poor, and with the needy of the city the unhappy Amir lined up for his portion. He looked upon the face of the angel who had taken his place, and the visage was so dazzling he had to look away. Daily the people began to respect the new Amir more for his kind actions, and the lessening of taxes, and his wisdom in adjudicating cases between those who brought lawsuits before him.

One night, the house where the beggar Amir was watching, waiting to go to sleep beside the oven when all the people were in bed, caught fire. He raised the alarm, and brought out two children who had been trapped in their room at the top of the house. He disappeared as soon as they were safe, and hid himself in a corner of the yard, where animals were being saddled for the dawn start of the caravan. In the night he had a dream, and thought himself to be the Amir again, but in the morning, as the beasts were snorting and stamping all around him, he found himself a beggar indeed.

That Friday, when he went with all the other needy ones to the Palace for his dole, he received it from the hand of the angel Amir, who smiled at him and said, 'Well done, servant of Allah, soon you shall recover what has been lost.' And then there was such a dazzling light from his countenance that the Amir had to look away.

Next day, when a runaway horse came stumbling through the streets, with its eyes wild and its mouth flecked with foam, the Amir who was a beggar stepped forward into the horse's path and stopped it, calming it with soothing words. Then the owner's servant came running up, praising his courage and calling blessings down upon his head. The people of the market all flooded round him: the fruit-vendor gave him oranges, and the sweetmeat-seller a pound of succulent hulwa, while from the upper windows of houses harem ladies showered coins around his feet. The sandal-maker made him accept a new pair of fine leather sandals, saying, 'Wear these, my friend, they are good enough for the Amir himself!' Everybody laughed and slapped him on the back, calling him a brave fellow.

Now, the former Amir was beginning to feel more human than he had done for many years, and he bitterly regretted all the injustices he had done when he was ruler in that place. He said aloud to himself, 'What fine people these are in my city. Would that I were their leader once more, for now that I know them and their trials, as I never did before, I would be considerate to all men, and respect them.'

No sooner were these words out of his mouth than the angel dressed as the Amir appeared before him and said,

'O servant of Allah, everything about you has now changed, and for the better. It is time that you returned to your rightful place. Go in Peace.'

Then the angel vanished, leaving a pile of finely made clothes and the ruby ring behind him. These the real Amir put on, and became once more his old self. He went to the gate of his Palace and ordered the guard to open it. This time the soldier bowed low and threw the gate open in a trice.

So the Amir returned a wiser man, and ruled his people justly for the rest of his days.

The Meatballs' Leader

Once upon a time, there was a dish of meatballs, sizzling in the oven.

'Oh, oh, oh, who will save us from this terrible scorching heat?' cried the meatballs.

'I will save you', said a large meatball in the middle of the tin, 'Think of me as your leader, and I can promise you beds of fine white rice upon which to lie, and a cooling sauce to cover your sizzling sides.'

So all the meatballs with one voice agreed to follow the large meatball in word and deed, and unanimously they chose him as their leader.

No sooner had the vote been taken, than the Cook opened the oven door and laid the meatballs upon large plates of gleaming white rice.

'O Excellent Meatball Leader,' they cried, as the Cook poured a rich, red tomato sauce upon them, 'You have indeed led us out of danger, into this cool, refreshing place of rice and sauce.'

But at that moment, several of the meatballs were forked onto plates, and felt themselves being swallowed by humans.

'Perfidious Meatball,' cried the remainder, 'You have led us into acute danger. How can you explain this horror and degradation which now faces us. You have deluded and deceived us, who gave you all our loyalty and devotion!'

'I knew that the next step in all our lives was from the oven onto cooling beds of rice,' said the large meatball, 'and look, even as I speak I go the way of all meatballs, for is it not our ultimate destiny to be eaten?' and he slipped down a human throat as easily as a meatball which has been chewed usually does.